The Gorillas of Gill Park

The Gorillas of Gill Park

By Amy Gordon

With illustrations by Matthew Cordell

SCHOLASTIC INC.

New York Toronto London Auckland Sydney
Mexico City New Delhi Hong Kong Buenos Aires

Many thanks to William Reid
for sharing his invaluable insights,
as well as his firsthand knowledge of baseball.

ISBN 0-439-64312-0

12 11 10 9 8 7 6 5 4 3 2 1   4 5 6 7 8 9/0

Printed in the U.S.A   40

First paperback printing, January 2004

For Larch

The Gorillas of Gill Park

one

The first thing you have to do every morning
is make your bed.

—*Marcia Wilson*

"He can't just hang around."

That was my mother, talking about me, and I was thinking, *Doesn't she know I'm right here in the living room, sitting right next to her?* As I sat and watched our goldfish swimming around and around in their bowl, I listened to her figure out how I was going to spend the summer.

"He needs to do *something,* you know that, Bill. We've got to get him out of the house and doing things with other kids."

"He could be a caddie for Ernie Johnson."

That was my father. He was sitting in his armchair, the newspaper he had been trying to read spread out on his knees. "Ernie's always looking for caddies and he pays well," he said, without looking up. My father was a lawyer and Ernie Johnson was my father's partner. I tried to imagine being Ernie Johnson's caddie all summer and decided it would be a lot like swimming around and around in a gold-fish bowl.

My father briskly shook out the paper and folded it up. "Or," he said, frowning slightly, "maybe Willy should go to summer school. So they'll let him into the seventh grade." He grunted, which was his way of laughing.

The goldfish kept swimming, around and around. Didn't they get bored? And I thought about how in sixth grade I was getting Cs in math and social studies and science. Maybe I *would* have to go to summer school.

"Well, there's camp, of course," my mother said. The legs of her gray slacks kept making me think of elephant legs. It wasn't that my mother was large or heavy; she was, in fact, *petite* (that's what all her friends said), but there was something large and heavy about her when she was trying to make decisions about me, her only child.

"There are all kinds of camps," she was saying. "I wonder what kind would be best for him? Hmmm, maybe some sort of sports camp to help him become more athletic." She cast her large brown eyes on me thoughtfully for the first time. "Or, I know just the thing. Music camp, so he can get *really* good on the violin."

The phone rang. My mother leaped up to answer it, and then she said, "You what? You want to speak to *Willy*? Willy, it's Aunt Bridget for you." She handed me the phone, then hovered over me because hardly anyone ever called for me.

"Willy? How're you doing?" Aunt Bridget's voice was warm and loud.

"I'm—I'm okay," I stammered. I found it difficult to talk with my parents' eyes riveted on me.

"What are your plans for the summer?" she asked.

"I don't know," I mumbled.

"How'd you like to come and stay with me in the big city of Gloria for a while? I have to make thirty gorilla suits this summer and I'm going to go nuts unless I have someone to keep me company."

I stammered back, "I'll—I'll ask my parents." *Gorilla* suits? *Thirty* gorilla suits? What would it be like to spend the summer with someone who was making thirty gorilla suits?

First my mother and then my father got on the phone, and after a lot of questions (mostly from my father), they told Aunt Bridget they would make a decision and call her back.

"Well," said my mother, looking bright and cheerful, as if she had already made up her mind, "Bridget would be fun for him. He needs to have some fun sometimes. I don't know why we didn't think of her before."

"I know why," my father said. He frowned again and began pacing around the room, jingling change in the pockets of his khaki pants. "Bridget isn't exactly . . . grown up."

My mother laughed. Her laugh sounded like, "Oh ho ho," which was to say, how amusing. "Everyone knows that people in the theater don't grow up, Bill."

"But Bridget is not in the theater," my father argued. "She just makes costumes *for* people in the theater."

"Same thing," said my mother.

"When we were kids, she was always making me dress up like a pirate or a cowboy or a gangster. Once I had to be Peter Pan! I had to wear *tights*! *Green* tights." My father's forehead wrinkled at the memory. "Most people outgrow that stuff, but I guess she never did."

"But, really," my mother asked, "what do you think, Bill?"

I stood very still, dizzy inside all the way to the pit of my stomach. Usually I didn't do a lot of new stuff because I was afraid to, but now . . . I *wanted* to go to Aunt Bridget's. She lived two and a half hours away, and we mostly only saw her and Uncle Roger for a short time at Christmas. When I was little, we'd gone to Gloria to their place, but one time my mother complained. She said it wasn't comfortable and if we were going to get together, they'd have to come to our place. Even if we'd lived closer, it was as if my father and Aunt Bridget lived on different planets. But hearing my aunt's voice on the phone reminded me of how much I liked her when I did see her—that warm, loud voice on the telephone . . . Something inside me woke up a little. Yes, Aunt

4

Bridget was a little loud, but she had a real laugh, not a ho-ho-ho-how-amusing laugh.

"She's probably lonely, Bill," my mother said. "I'm sure she misses Roger."

My father nodded and sighed. "Well, yes, that's true. That's a tragedy all right."

A few months before, my uncle Roger had died of cancer. I had never known him that well, but I was sorry because he had seemed like a fun, nice guy. He was tall and friendly and he always gave me presents my mother didn't approve of, like one year it was a potato gun—you could shoot little potato pellets out of this plastic gun—and another year it was a toy microphone that could distort your voice and it really drove my parents crazy.

Now my father shook his head. "Gloria is a big city—do you think he can handle himself there?" He took a pen from his shirt pocket and clicked the end of it. My father always did that, as if he were about to sign an important document or something.

"Bridget lives next to a nice park—it seems fairly safe there," my mother said.

"Well, we have to be sure she'll sit him down with school books a couple of nights each week."

"Oh, relax, Bill," my mother said. "We're not trying to get him into Harvard next year, you know."

"Not next year," my father said seriously, and he poked the pen back into his pocket.

two

Life automatically becomes more fun
if you give things names.
—*Roger McTaggart*

We had that conversation in March. My parents almost changed their minds twenty times between then and the end of school, but finally June came and my mother and I were actually in the car headed for Gloria. "Now you be a *help* to Bridget," my mother said. The two-and-a-half-hour drive gave her a nice long amount of time to nag me. "And don't let her spend a lot of money on you. I'm sure things are hard on her since Roger died. Be sure to offer to vacuum and wash dishes. You don't want to burden her."

I sighed and looked out the window. Was I going to burden Aunt Bridget? Why had she invited me if I was going to be such a burden? Maybe because she felt sorry for me, an only child with busy parents, not so many friends, not so good at things. . . .

"And you help out with those gorillas."

I turned slightly to see if Mom was smiling at all as she said this, but no, she looked as earnest as an elephant.

It was almost dark when we arrived. I opened the car door to warm and grimy end-of-the-day city smells. My aunt lived on the second floor of a two-story walk-up. I carried my suitcase up the creaky old wooden stairs.

"Hello, I hear you coming," Aunt Bridget called down. I felt a slight thrill at the sound of her voice. And then she appeared on the stairs above me. She looked hot and sweaty and her black hair was even curlier than usual. She was wearing a bright orange blouse and blue jeans. "Willy!" she exclaimed as she grabbed the suitcase from me. "Look at you!" She stared at me so hard I blushed. "You are *enormous*! I mean, I think you've grown ten inches more since the last time I saw you. Come on in, and please excuse the mess, everything is covered with gorilla fuzz." She looked down at her blouse, which I could now see had a film of black hairs all over it. "You can't believe how much this stuff sheds."

Aunt Bridget pushed me into the apartment. I backed into a corner, where I bumped into a body thing that didn't have arms or legs.

"What—what is that?" I asked.

"It's a dressmaker's form—you can build a cos-tume on it without having to use a real body," Aunt

Bridget said, and then her eyes crinkled as she smiled. "Actually, you should be asking, *who* is that. Roger used to call her Flora—he thought she looked rather Victorian."

I took a deep breath and looked around. Her apartment looked even smaller and more cramped and crowded than I had remembered. In front of me, taking up most of the small living room, was a table with a sewing machine on one end of it and stacks of black fuzzy stuff on the other.

"Am I glad you're here, Willy. These gorillas are turning me into a raving lunatic," said Aunt Bridget. "Your father, of course, thinks I am one—a raving lunatic, that is. Isn't that right, Willy?" She laughed. "It's okay, you don't have to answer."

Mom appeared in the door, holding the backpack with my summer reading books in one hand and my violin case in the other. "Wouldn't want to forget these," she said brightly.

"Marcia," my aunt greeted her warmly. "Thank you so much for loaning me Willy for the summer. It's really kind of you to let him go for such a long time. How about some lemonade, now, both of you, after such a long, hot drive?"

"We do have air conditioning, of course," Mom said, and she did look as cool as a cucumber compared to Aunt Bridget, who looked like a sweaty orange. "And thank you, anyway, but I ought to be heading home."

"Home?" Aunt Bridget looked aghast at my mother. "But my guest room is all set."

"Well, I just didn't want to burden you. I know you don't have much room here, and besides, I have to do a luncheon for Bill tomorrow so I'd have to get up awfully early anyway to get back in time."

There was an awkward silence for a moment. Then Aunt Bridget put back her head and laughed. "Suit yourself," she said.

Mom handed her an envelope. "This should help you out, and Bridget, thanks so much again for having him." Turning to me, she said, "And you have a wonderful time, Willy, and don't forget to be a *help*." She emphasized the word *help* for the hundredth time. "Bye bye, sweetie." She put her arms around me and pecked me on the cheek. As I watched her white legs disappear down the creaking wooden stairs (she was wearing white slacks that day), I thought, *Wow, she's leaving, just like that.*

I hadn't been away from home much before, not for more than a night or two. Mom hadn't seemed that sad about leaving me, but I had a funny feeling in my throat. Here I was, alone with my aunt. I stared at her, shyness creeping up from my toes.

Aunt Bridget looked back at me and then down at herself. "Well, I am a bit disheveled. I must have scared her away. And maybe she's allergic to gorilla hair. She certainly couldn't wait to get out of here."

"I don't think it was you," I said apologetically, feeling even worse now about how quickly my mother had left, not just for myself, but for my aunt.

"I wonder," she said, a line appearing between her thick black eyebrows. "I know why she left so quickly. She's gonna miss you, Willy boy, and she didn't want to blubber all over you. She was being stoic."

Okay, I thought, that was it. That pinched look on my mother's face.

"Now, me, I would have slobbered all over you and embarrassed you to death. Well, come on, Willy, my friend, let me show you the bathroom first and then where you'll be staying." She nudged me out of the living room and into a narrow hallway. At the end of it was a small bathroom. "There it is, my lovely bathroom. It's not the Ritz, but for some reason, the water pressure's great in the shower. And here," she said, opening a door next to the bathroom, "is your room. It happens to be where I store a lot of costumes, but it has a terrific view of the park, so I know you won't mind."

I stared at rows of cardboard cartons stacked neatly against two of the walls. Some were marked with intriguing labels: ANIMAL MASKS, BLOOMERS AND KNICKERS, GYPSY NOTIONS, CAPES AND KINGS' ROBES. Next to a window was the bed with a colorful quilt made up of hundreds of patches of all shapes and sizes, and against another wall, near the door, was a bureau.

"I know you must have a bigger room at home," said Aunt Bridget, "but it's not as if you're going to be living here forever."

"I like it," I said, and I couldn't help the grin that spread across my face. The room felt private and secret, like a cave; it suited me. And best of all, there was a big white cat sleeping on the bed. We only had goldfish at home, goldfish swimming around and around in a bowl, because my mother was allergic to pet dander.

"Meet Sophie," said my aunt, scooping up the cat. I stroked her soft white head and the big cat purred. Then Aunt Bridget knelt on the bed and peered out the window. "Come and look, Willy," she said. "You can see the park fountain. It's all lit up at night."

I knelt on the bed beside her and looked. At first, all I could see was the shadowy street below, the parked cars, and the streetlamps casting lemony pools on the cracked sidewalk. But then, from out of the darkness, a sort of mysterious darkness that must have been the park, plumes of color shot up like fireworks in graceful slow motion.

"There it goes," said Aunt Bridget, resting her elbows on the windowsill. "Red, red, red, green, green, green, yellow, yellow, yellow, blue. You know how it is when you watch a thing that has a definite pattern—a rhythm gets set up inside your head and pretty soon it seems as if your heart is beating along in time to it, too."

I watched the pattern of the changing colors for a moment and I could see what she meant, but I was feeling something else, too, as if there were some-thing exciting out there in that blur of black. "I wish I could see more," I said, squinting.

Aunt Bridget laughed a hearty ha-ha-ha laugh, not an oh-ho-ho-how-amusing laugh. "You can go exploring first thing in the morning," she said. "Right when you wake up and hear the music."

"What music?" I asked, wondering if she was talking about an alarm clock radio.

"Oh, no, no, I'm not going to tell you about it," she said. She uncurled from the window and got up off the bed and looked at me with her hands on her hips. I sat back from the window, too, and stared at her. She was making her eyebrows jump up and down on her forehead. "The mystery of Gill Park music," she said in a whisper. "And now, Willy, I shall leave you so you can get settled." She waggled her eyebrows once more and then left the room.

three

I don't use a pattern when I sew—I just
eyeball things and figure out my own design.
—*Bridget McTaggart*

I did not jump out of bed in the morning. I had
stayed up late, because Aunt Bridget hadn't told me
when to go to bed. Before that, though, she had
ordered in Chinese food for supper. She was surprised to learn that I had never had Chinese food,
and as we sat in her small kitchen where one whole
wall was decorated with hats and canes and walking
sticks, I was surprised to find out how much I liked it.

After we had scraped the last bit of rice from the
squishy cardboard cartons, she said, "I'm going to
work some more, but you make yourself at home."
She showed me where my towels were in the bathroom and then squeezed my arm and said she was

glad I was there, so I went into the secret cave bedroom and stayed up and poked through the boxes.

There were all kinds of hats: cowboy and bowler and golf, and a top hat, a pirate hat with a skull and crossbones across the front of it, a sun bonnet, and a hat with peacock feathers all over it. The best one was a gangster type, gray, with a band around it. I put it on. "Hey, Jimmy, c'mere and look at dese shoes," I said. I was trying to talk like Marlon Brando in *The Godfather*. "Lookit all dese shoes." There were sandals, slippers, cowboy boots, silvery high heels. "And lookit all dese gloves." There were black ones with sequins and a bright green pair. Another box had capes and another one had vests and then there were a bunch of plastic bags labeled JAMES AND THE GIANT PEACH: SPIDER, LADYBUG, et cetera. Wow. I forgot about talking like Marlon Brando. What a great life my aunt Bridget had!

So now I lay dozing in bed, with the sunlight streaming in across the colorful quilt (Aunt Bridget hadn't told me when to get up, either); my ears filled with city sounds, of grinding gears and honking cars, of birds, even, outside the window, which all blended together to create a sort of city hum. Then I became aware of another sound that seemed to rise above everything else.

I hitched myself up on one elbow to look out the window. Directly below was the street, with lampposts and parked cars, and just across, on the other side, was the park. By daylight, it had lost the magic of the night before, but still it looked inviting, with green grass and park benches, and I could see kids skateboarding and riding bicycles. Further in was the fountain, but by day there were no plumes of color shooting up from it.

Then I heard the sound again. It was music. I pushed up the window and stuck out my head. It was crashing away, that music. I thought it might be a trumpet. It made me think of a king with his head held high, and all the people of the land marching behind him, but I couldn't tell where it was coming from. I craned my neck out farther. At first the sound seemed to be coming from everywhere, but then I had the impression it was coming from the park.

"Get up, get up," the music seemed to say. "Get up and march for the king."

I climbed out of bed, and, still in my pajamas, wandered into the living room, where Aunt Bridget was standing at her worktable in a pink bathrobe with black hair all over it. She was holding a pair of scissors.

"Oh, hello," she said when she saw me. "Sleep well?"

"I'm sorry—I didn't mean to sleep so late," I mumbled.

"What's to be sorry?" Aunt Bridget said cheerfully. With the back of her arm, she pushed back her hair, and I could see it was beginning to turn white around her ears. "I'm not going anywhere. Look at this stuff, Willy. Thirty gorillas. Can you imagine such a thing?"

"Someone's playing the trumpet and it's really loud but I can't tell where it's coming from," I said. I moved to the other end of the room, where there was a window overlooking the park, and stood listening. Aunt Bridget left her fuzz and came and stood beside me.

"Isn't it wonderful!" she exclaimed happily. "The only park in the world that has live music all the time."

"Live music?" I asked. "Who's playing it?"

"Ah, the mystery of Gill Park music," she said, eyebrows waggling again. "But I'll let you in on the secret, Willy. He lives over there." She pointed with her scissors. "Across the park."

"Who does?"

"Otto Pettingill." A trumpet note blasted just as she said his name. "Huh, how about that? He's playing the trumpet. I can't remember the last time he played the trumpet. Must be in honor of your arrival, Willy."

"He knows I'm here?"

"I'm just kidding, actually," said Aunt Bridget. "But it's amazing how the music fits into what you're doing."

"But who is he?" I asked her again.

"Otto Pettingill is the owner of Gill Park and he is a musician. So, he has an amplifier in his apartment and speakers hooked up all over the trees in the park. It's wild, it really is, when you think about it," she said, looking pleased. "Sometimes he plays Bach on the violin, or sometimes it'll be jazz. He also plays the clarinet and the oboe, and oh, I don't know, the cello and viola and nearly anything you could name. Lately it's been the piano or strings."

"Holy cow," I said. "Why?"

"Why what?"

"Why does he do it?"

Aunt Bridget shook her head as she walked back to her worktable and began cutting fuzz again. Little black hairs rained from the scissors as she cut. "Why does he do it? That's the mystery. We really don't know why, but most of us have grown so used to it, we've stopped asking why." She shook her head again. "No one ever sees him. He's filthy rich, you know—he can do what he likes. He's eccentric, marches to a different drummer—"

"I know what *eccentric* means," I said. "Dad—" But then I stopped, feeling myself turn red and I couldn't go on.

Aunt Bridget laughed her hearty ho-ho-ho laugh. "You mean," she said, "one time you asked what *eccentric* means and your father said, 'You know, like your aunt Bridget and uncle Roger.'" She lowered her voice and frowned, just the way my father frowns, and paced just the way he always does, with his hands crammed into his pockets. She looked a lot like him, only a funnier version, like a cartoon, and I couldn't help laughing; and then my stomach growled, and then Aunt Bridget laughed with me.

"Better feed you," she said. "Come on." I trailed after her into the kitchen. She opened the refrigerator and stood in front of it a minute before saying, "This is a disaster. All I have is a one-hundred-year-old carrot and dying garlic leaves moldering to an empty bread bag and a slimy butter dish. Ever notice how butter dishes get slimy in the fridge?"

"I don't actually get that close to the inside of refrigerators," I said.

Aunt Bridget shut the door and stood staring at me, and then she burst out laughing. "You are a riot," she said. "An absolute riot." I shifted uncomfortably from foot to foot. I hadn't been aware of trying to be funny, but I couldn't help being pleased she thought I had been.

"Tell you what, Will, why don't you get dressed and then run over to Rosa's Market and get us some groceries. We need milk, that's all I know for sure." She stuck her fingers into a cracked green mug that was on top of the refrigerator. "Oh ouch and damn," she yelped, hopping around the kitchen, sticking her fingers in her mouth. "Fishhooks," she mumbled between fingers. "I always forget."

"Fishhooks?" I asked.

"I put Roger's fishhooks in the money cup and I always forget."

"But why don't you take them out?"

"It's a way of not forgetting him," she said. "Not that I'm likely to." I looked down at my feet because the thought of Uncle Roger not being alive anymore made shyness creep all through me again. "Get dressed and then take this twenty," Aunt Bridget said, waving a crumpled green bill at me.

"What do you want me to get?" I asked, panic replacing shyness.

"Oh, you decide," she said. "That's why you're here—so I don't have to make decisions like that. Okay, Willy, my boy, off you go because I have to get back to work."

I threw on a T-shirt and jeans, feeling increasingly worried. I had never, never, never in my whole life decided what I was going to eat. "Where is Rosa's?" I asked, coming out to the table, hating to bother my aunt, who was hunkered over the fuzz again.

"Oh, just turn left when you get outside and two blocks down turn left again and you can take a shortcut through the little alley and then Rosa's is across the street you come out on, diagonally to the right. You'll see fruits and vegetables piled out in front and there's a nice green-and-white striped awning and it says Rosa's—"

There was a wild banging on the door.

Aunt Bridget looked up and then sighed. "Oh, so much for work," she said. "It's Gareth Pugh come to draft you as a first baseman. I forgot to tell you this might happen. Open the door for him, will you?"

four

Anyone can play baseball
and be good at it.

—*Gareth Pugh*

A skinny boy burst into the apartment. His baseball glove appeared first and the rest of him followed. A dark blue baseball cap was jammed down over his eyes. "Hey, Bridget!" He barreled toward her, shaking the glove at her. "So, can the nephew play?" His mouth was so full of braces his lower jaw seesawed as he spoke. His whole body seemed to vibrate as if there were little jumping beans zipping about underneath his skin. Even his freckles seemed to be jumping around on his nose.

"Willy, this is Gareth, baseball coach extraordinaire; and Gareth, this is Willy, the nephew."

"Little League acts like it owns the place; we have to squeeze practices between their practices, so let's go," said Gareth, pointing his glove at me. I stared at him. He reminded me of an insect. His skinny arms wavered in the air like antennae. And then I swallowed hard. If Gareth were a bug, then I, Willy, was a turtle—I could feel myself pulling right into my shell. I hated baseball. Detested it. Loathed it. I was one of those kids at school the coach sticks out in right field because most kids can't hit the ball out that far. "I don't have a glove," I said.

"Hey, no problem," said Gareth. He hadn't seemed to notice my lack of enthusiasm. "You can use my glove. I don't play. I coach."

"He means *boss,* don't let him kid you," said Aunt Bridget, waggling her eyebrows.

"Okay, buddy, let's go," Gareth said, ignoring her. "Like I said, we have to grab the moment."

"Get something to eat on your way so you don't faint," Aunt Bridget said as Gareth pushed me out the door. "And don't forget to go to Rosa's on the way back—just get milk and then what you like and don't worry about it—you still have that twenty?"

I found myself out on the street, walking, or running, really, in order to keep up with Gareth, and then as we passed through a pair of iron gates into Gill Park, *zap zap zap,* an electric shock went through me. It wasn't a scary shock like the time when I was little and had stuck a finger in a socket and thought I was going to die right there on the spot; no, it was a different kind of shock: I felt myself grow bigger and taller and the molecules that made up my body felt zippier.

To look around, nothing seemed out of the ordinary. There were benches and birds, and an old lady was warming herself in the sun. A couple sat on the grass changing their baby's diaper. There was a statue of a soldier on a horse, sword held high. COLONEL OLIVER PETTINGILL, ADJUTANT TO THEODORE ROOSEVELT, the plaque on the monument said. Men looking just like my dad—they were all decked out in dark business suits—walked briskly by, carrying their briefcases, and mothers wheeled their babies around.

But that trumpet was still playing, and I knew it was the music that was making my molecules feel zippier. It made me think I might even enjoy playing baseball—but then, with a sinking heart, I remembered Gareth wanted me to play first base. First base? I wasn't too sure about that. It was my duty to tell Gareth I wasn't so hot.

"I never played first base before, you know," I said.

Gareth stopped in front of a pretzel vendor. "Want one?" he asked.

Breaking the twenty Aunt Bridget had given me, I bought a pretzel. It was warm and fresh and I thought the music was making even the food in the park taste good.

"Did you hear what I said about not having ever played first base?" I mumbled through a bite.

"Yeah, I heard." Gareth shrugged and spread out his skinny arms.

"Why would you want me?" I couldn't help asking. "I mean, there must be tons of kids around here you could get to play first base."

Gareth shook his head. "We're not a Little League team," he said. "Most of the kids who want to play ball around here are in Little League."

So you're desperate, I wanted to say, but Gareth jumped in before I had a chance. "You are intelligent, aren't you? All you have to be is intelligent to play first base." I couldn't help smiling. Gareth made everything seem easy. I wondered how old he was. He was tall, but even so, he didn't look that old—maybe he had just finished seventh grade—but *intelligent* wasn't a word most kids used. Why wasn't I just saying *No, I'm not going to play for you?*

"Are—are you playing a game today?" I asked nervously.

"Just practicing," said Gareth, pretzel pushing around in his braces. He didn't really chew—he mashed. "But pretty soon we play the Sharks."

"Are—are they good?"

"Very good," Gareth said seriously. "One of the best nonleague teams in the park. There are a couple of nonleagues, but they're kind of shabby, except for us and the Sharks. Man, they beat us every year. It's because of their pitcher, Dillon Deronda. But we've got a good chance, now you're here. We're depending on you."

"Depending on *me*?" Why wasn't I home with Mom and Dad and a house free of pet dander? Home, watching the goldfish.

Gareth didn't seem to hear me. "You understand

why I don't play Little League?" he asked, pausing slightly in his mashing.

"Um, no," I said.

"Even though I'm the best kid player in this park, I don't want to play. I want to coach and manage. Little League won't let me do that. So my dad said, 'If you want to coach and manage, you should do it,' so that's what I'm doing. Of course, it's tough to get practice time on the field. And almost impossible to get a uniform." Gareth wiped soggy bits of pretzel off his mouth with his baseball glove.

"Maybe my aunt could make you some," I said. "When she's finished the gorillas."

Gareth turned and slugged me enthusiastically on the arm, a hefty, friendly punch. "Hey, now that's a brilliant idea! I knew it! I knew you were intelligent!" His eyes shone. "We need something to intimidate those Sharks. Baseball's all in the brain, you know. But come on, I can't be late. My dad says it sets a bad example."

He strode off and I followed. We passed a flower stand, where a tall thin man was arranging flowers in buckets. "Hey, Mitch," Gareth called as we passed by. "Want to know what I figured out?"

We paused for a moment, while the tall thin man rubbed his head, which was full of gray, very springy hair, and looked at Gareth with great interest.

"I figured out why cut flowers smell so much stronger than flowers that are still growing. It's cuz they're sweating—they're sweating cuz they have to work so hard to stay alive."

"Hmmm," said Mitch. He had a very noticeable Adam's apple, and it sort of bobbed as he spoke. "I'll have to think about that one, Gareth."

"That's Mitch Bloom," Gareth said as we walked away. "He told me once he always knew he'd do something with plants because of his name. Now what would I end up doing if I did something to do with *my* last name?"

"Raise skunks," I said.

"Clean sewers," said Gareth.

"Recycle basketball shoes."

"Grow rotten eggs."

"Can you *grow* rotten eggs?" I asked.

We passed a bench where an amazingly wrinkled old woman sat talking to herself. "That's Old Violet," said Gareth, pushing me past her. "Come on, keep walking fast or she'll grab you and say, 'What a big boy you are, *ha!*' And then she'll tell you how her dentist fell in love with her and gave her free dentures. And over there's Jerry Rabinowitz." He pointed to a man sitting on another bench with piles and piles of books and papers all around him. "He writes poetry, and every single one of his poems has the word *green* in it. He's cool, but we don't have time for him today."

The last bit of pretzel lodged in my throat. We were approaching the baseball field, and I could see kids swinging bats and tossing balls. Even if this wasn't Little League, it was way more than a casual backyard game.

"Hey, guys!" Gareth waved his arms in the air. "I got us a first baseman."

The kids came crowding up, and I could feel my legs beginning to shake. "Here's the team, Willy," Gareth said. "Hoscowitz is the pitcher and Toenail is shortstop." He rattled off the rest of the players, pointing to them as he named the positions.

The kids seemed to come in all shapes and colors and sizes, but I was too nervous to take in most of the information (although the name Toenail stuck, and besides that, his hair was blue), until Gareth got to the third baseman. "Liesl Summer," Gareth said, and I wasn't likely to forget her. I had never seen anyone who looked as strange as she did.

five

Either a thing is dumb or cool—
there isn't anything in between.

—*Liesl Summer*

Liesl Summer was small and skinny and she had a tough little face underneath a very faded baseball cap. It might have been red once, or orange, it was hard to tell—now it was sort of the color of tonsils. She was wearing a red-and-white-checked blouse, a long red skirt, a blue apron with deep pockets in it, and very holey, very dirty red sneakers.

She narrowed her eyes at me. "Can you play?" she asked suspiciously.

I wanted to say, *No way can I play,* but Gareth was yelling at everyone to get onto the field. I was wondering who was going to bat when I saw Gareth step up to the plate and start swinging. "Okay,

Hoscowitz," he called out to the pitcher. "Drive 'em at me, baby."

I stood near first base, wishing I could turn to someone, maybe Hoscowitz, and say, *Look, I really don't know what I'm doing here,* but Hoscowitz was chomping on a piece of gum, looking very serious as he wound up to pitch to Gareth. All I could do was watch, feeling like the biggest phony in the universe, wondering how long it was going to take for me to be humiliated.

As Gareth swung the bat, I could see right away he was hot stuff. I'd never seen a kid swing a bat so gracefully or hit the ball so powerfully. I never would have guessed that such a skinny kid could pack such a wallop.

The ball spun out toward the second baseman, who reached for it, caught it, but then dropped it. I felt a sneaking relief—maybe these kids weren't total pros.

"For Pete's sake, Dixon," Gareth growled. "We're not chasing butterflies out here today."

By the time a couple more kids had either dropped the ball or had thrown it to the wrong place, and Gareth yelled at the catcher: "Come on, Capasso, what'd ya do, grease your fingers with butter this morning?" I was feeling much better. Not exactly cocky, but not as if I was about to throw up, either. If and when the ball ever came my way, maybe I wouldn't make a complete fool of myself.

And the ball did come my way. I scooped it up easily and put out my glove to tap Gareth, who was running full tilt at me.

"Way to go, Wilson!" Gareth yelled, leaping wildly.

Hoscowitz came over and whacked me on the back and the other kids whistled and yelled. Everyone was happy except Liesl Summer, who stood by third base and didn't move a muscle except to spit. I didn't care about her, though. I slapped my fist into the glove like a seasoned player. So what was the big deal about baseball, anyway?

Gareth went back to the plate and smacked another ball right at me. I ducked my head, jammed my glove up at the last minute, and the ball rushed by.

"Come on, Wilson!" Gareth fumed. "Don't hide from the ball. Think it's gonna wreck your beautiful face or something?"

Maybe baseball *was* a big deal. My face burning, I glanced over at Liesl and saw her standing with her arms crossed and a see-I-told-you expression on her face.

But all of a sudden, piano music filled my ears. I knew enough about music to know it was ragtime, and I couldn't help feeling happy. I realized it was summer, and I was free from school, and the warm air was filled with the smell of popcorn and cotton candy, and I was playing baseball with a whole new group of kids who didn't know I was a total loser.

I was amazed that music could be like this. At home, music was torture. My mother made me play the violin, thinking if I wasn't athletic, I must be musical. The way I was being taught, a parent was supposed to learn with you, and of course my dad didn't want to have anything to do with a violin. So there we'd be, my mom and I, scraping and squealing away, and now and then I would glance sideways at her and be distracted by the double chins she'd get from holding the violin. It wasn't exactly beautiful music we were making.

Gareth popped another ball past my right ear. I was ready. There was a satisfying thud in my glove. "Now over to third!" Gareth yelled. I flung the ball over to Liesl. Her arm shot up in the air, but the ball only rocked in her glove for a moment before it fell to the ground with a plop.

Gareth jumped up and down like a wild man. "What's the matter with you, Summer? Too much chalk on your hands or what?"

Liesl stared at Gareth as red blotches blazed on her face. Then she began to scream back at him. "Gareth Pugh, shut your stinking big mouth. I'm sick of you yelling at me every time I drop the stupid ball." She tore the baseball cap off her head and slammed it to the ground. A snarled-up mess of dirty yellow hair tumbled down around her face. Gareth took off his cap and swiped an arm across his eyes. *His* hair was plastered to his skull, and it looked as if he had permanent cap dents in his head.

"Here we go," he groaned. "Another practice wrecked because of her stupid tantrums."

The piano stopped suddenly. Another instrument took its place and started playing quieter, more melancholy music. Gradually I realized it was a violin—it sounded a thousand times better than anything I ever played, and it was funny how it seemed to go with what was going on, like the musical score of a movie. I looked in the direction Aunt Bridget had pointed to earlier and saw a row of apartment buildings facing the park. Was Mr. Pettingill watching from his window?

Liesl stormed away, and the other teammates, all boys, gathered around Gareth.

"Hey, man," Capasso, the catcher, said. "We don't have to put up with that freak."

Gareth sighed. "She's a genius of a third baseman. She's got good hands, good reflexes, and a good arm. They don't come any better."

"She acts like she's five years old," said Dixon.

"More like three," said Hoscowitz. "My little brother is five and he acts more mature than that."

"Okay, guys, that's enough," said Gareth. "Let's get back to work. Toenail, you take third."

The little guy with blue hair who had been playing shortstop stepped forward and nodded. The rest of us went back to our positions, and the practice lasted another hour. We never practiced hitting at all, and I was relieved. Standing in the field was one thing, hitting was another.

At the end, the boys passed by me, some nodding in my direction, saying, "Later, Wilson," or, "See ya, buddy, good job," and I almost felt like one of the guys. Then I looked around, wondering what I would do next. Explore the park? I wanted to figure out exactly which building it was that the music was coming from.

I didn't have a chance to, though. Gareth grabbed me. "Hey, Willy, I'll take you to Rosa's—it's the least I can do in return for you playing pretty good today."

I allowed myself to be dragged along by Gareth; I couldn't help liking the guy, even if he was incredibly bossy.

six

When I come into my store in the
early morning, I breathe in the smell of
my fruit and my vegetables and the smell
of the old wooden floors, and the scent of
this lady's perfume and that man's sweat,
and that little child's stickiness on a hot
summer day, and I have to tell you, I am happy.
—*Rosa, of Rosa's Market*

"I was sort of expecting to see my dad," Gareth said
as we walked. "Sometimes he sneaks out of the office
for half an hour so he can watch practice and give
me some pointers."

I looked at Gareth with awe and admiration—to *want* to have your father show up! At my school, they didn't believe in cuts or anything like that, so I *had* to play sports—soccer in the fall, basketball in the winter, baseball in the spring. During a game, I always knew the exact moment my father arrived to watch me. Out of the corner of my eye I'd see the tall man in a suit join my mother, and there they'd be, the two of them, tall and short, standing apart from the other parents. I don't know why they always stood apart, not chatting and gossiping with other people, but anyway, I'd usually be playing okay until Dad arrived; then suddenly the ball would roll underneath my feet and I'd fall, or the soccer ball would bounce off me and I'd make a goal for the wrong team. In basketball, I'd get confused as to which way we were going and make a basket for the other team (most valuable player—for the *other* team, Dad joked, heh heh). In baseball the one time they let me pitch, a kid hit a ball straight at me. I took it on the mouth and cracked a tooth and it had hurt so bad, and ever since I was afraid of the ball, and the coach always stuck me out in right field.

"And when Dad's there, Liesl's less likely to lose it," Gareth was saying glumly.

"Who is she, anyway?" I asked. "She seems really . . . really—"

"Weird," Gareth said for me. "But like I said, she's a great third baseman, nothing wimpy about her, so I don't want to fire her."

Personally, I thought Gareth could improve the

way he talked to his players. I was amazed more of them didn't walk off the field the way Liesl had. But then I remembered how Gareth had hit the ball, making contact with it every time, no matter what the pitch was like, and he had also been able to direct it exactly where he wanted. Maybe the other kids really respected Gareth—they knew they were working with a pro.

"But she's not like you," said Gareth, leading the way out of the park and along the sidewalk. "She can't take criticism. How's she supposed to get better if she can't take a little heat?"

"Yeah, it's great to be yelled at," I said, feeling myself go red at the compliment. The kids at home didn't yell at me, I realized; they just ignored me because they had given up on me. If Gareth yelled at me, maybe it meant he thought I was capable of doing better. "But where does that girl come from?" I asked. "Why does she look like that?"

"The story of Liesl Summer is a strange tale," Gareth said dramatically. "Her parents died in a car crash when she was little, and then Otto Pettingill adopted her. He set her up in an apartment over there"—he nodded back in the direction we had come from—"and a retired old schoolteacher lives with her and takes care of her, but she's not allowed to pick clothes out for Liesl or anything, or tell her what to do, and Liesl isn't allowed to go to school. She hangs around the park all day drawing on the pavement with chalk. That's why I made that crack about her hands being all chalky."

I stopped walking and stared at Gareth. "Holy cow," I said. "She's not allowed to go to school? How does she get to be so lucky?"

"My dad says Otto Pettingill has this philosophy about how kids should be raised. But I don't think she's so lucky," he said, frowning, a line appearing between his eyebrows. "I wouldn't like not going to school, but then, I'm the best student in my class."

I couldn't help smiling. Gareth certainly didn't mind talking about how good he was at things. "But isn't there a law you have to go to school?" I asked.

"Otto Pettingill must have found a way of getting around it," Gareth said. "Don't ask me how. She does her own shopping and cooking and she gets to choose what she does every day," said Gareth. "I guess you could say she's an experiment."

"Holy cow," I said again. "This Otto Pettingill—my aunt told me about how he plays music all the time."

Gareth shrugged. "I don't even hear it half the time. I guess I'm too used to it. Here's Rosa's," he said, stopping in front of a store with a green-and-white-striped awning hanging brightly over boxes of fruit and vegetables.

We stepped into the store and I looked around at the shelves. "I don't know what to get," I said, the panicky feeling starting again.

"Hey, your aunt said you should get what you like," said Gareth.

"I don't know what I like."

Gareth quivered indignantly, his freckles bouncing. "You *have* to know what you like." He stopped in front of a jar of olives. "Get these," he said.

I shuddered. "I hate olives."

"Well, at least you know what you *don't* like."

"I like those," I said, eyeing a bin of kiwis.

"Twenty dollars' worth of kiwis," Gareth said, making a move toward them.

"Wait a minute," I said. "We should get coffee. Aunt Bridget was drinking coffee this morning and I bet she always runs out of it. And she said milk, so we should get milk. And we should get cereal."

I hunted until I found the cereals, and then I saw the little boxes of sweet cereals, the kind my mother never bought. I'd always wanted those. *Willy, Willy, buy me,* they were calling. I reached up and put a whole package of them (there were twelve of them, bound together in plastic) in my basket. I was jealous of Liesl Summer—she got to do this every day of her life.

That just about exhausted my great daring. All I could think of then was boring stuff like bread and butter. And cat food.

"For Sophie," I said to Gareth.

"Pretty good," said Gareth. "Even I wouldn't have remembered pet food. And don't forget the kiwis."

"Look at this!" Aunt Bridget exclaimed in admiration after we staggered into the apartment with the grocery bags and she started helping unload. "Kiwis! I love kiwis! And cat food! Sophie will bless you forever! And coffee! And bread! And cute little cereal boxes. I made beds for my dolls with these when I was little. And milk! Why, Willy, you have a practical head on your shoulders!"

I shrugged happily. What was the big deal about grocery shopping anyway?

"You like green olives?" she asked, pulling out a bottle. "And canned peas?"

"Me," said Gareth. "I do. For when I come over." He took the bottle of olives and opened it. "Want some?"

I backed away. "They taste like frogs' eyes," I said in disgust.

"Oh, so how often have you had frogs' eyes?" Gareth asked.

Aunt Bridget put back her head and laughed, and then I laughed, and the music—it was a crazy tune on the violin now—Otto Pettingill was playing it like a fiddle—a jig or something like that—it bounced in through the open window, making me want to leap around like a wild man.

seven

A person's face goes in your eyes
and down your arms and into your fingers,
and that's how you draw.

—*Liesl Summer*

I woke up on the second morning listening for the music. There it was, beating a path through the noise of the traffic. It was piano again today, a slow, lazy, peaceful rhythm, making me feel like staying in bed all day.

I got up and found my aunt bending over the sewing table. She was wearing the pink bathrobe, which seemed to have even more black hairs all over it. "Think this stuff will eventually turn Sophie the white cat into a black cat?" she asked, and I smiled and thought about how my mother would hate all this hair. She would have been vacuuming every few minutes.

"Help yourself to breakfast; after all, you bought it," said Aunt Bridget. "Poor Roger, when we were first married, he didn't realize what he'd gotten himself into, a domestically disabled wife, but he figured out pretty fast that if we were going to eat he'd have to be the chef." She sighed. "And a great one he was, too. Trouble was, you see, I grew up in a house with an army of servants. They'd come in and say, 'Breakfast is served.' Or, 'Luncheon is served.' They always said things like that in the same way."

I nodded. I knew Dad and Aunt Bridget had been super rich when they were growing up. Then somehow my grandfather lost a lot of money and they weren't super rich anymore, just regular.

"I never made a bed in my life when I was growing up. The servants always made it. Isn't that terrible?"

"I don't know," I said, thinking about how my mother made me make my bed every morning. "Isn't it dumb to make your bed, because you're just going to mess it up anyway?"

"But if you don't make it, after a while the sheets get all pulled out and then they take on a life of their own—they grab you in the middle of the night and wrap around you." She held up the black fuzz, which now had a shape, like a pair of fuzzy black pajamas. "What do you think, Willy? Gorilla suit numero uno. I think I'm getting the hang of this, and pretty soon this place'll be a gorilla suit factory. The next twenty-nine should be a snap. Speaking of snaps, though—I may not be able to put a zipper in these."

I was trying to follow Aunt Bridget's train of thought when the phone rang.

"You get it, please, Willy," said Aunt Bridget.

It was my mother. "Are you having a good time, sweetie?" she wanted to know. I found I had more to talk about than usual. I told her how I was playing first base and that there was a man who played music into the park all day long and there was a girl who didn't have to go to school.

"How interesting," my mother said, but I thought she sounded a little flat and I wondered how interested she really was. "Have you done any of your summer reading yet, and have you practiced the violin?"

"Not yet," I admitted.

"Well, the whole summer's going to fly by and you don't want to leave it for the end; and you've got to keep those scales going, you'll forget everything if you don't."

"Not such a hot conversation, eh?" Aunt Bridget said, eyeing me as I hung up.

"I wish I could live like Liesl Summer," I said. I felt as if someone had stuck me all over with pins. I felt like a dead balloon. I *hated* how I felt after talking to my mother.

"Liesl Summer, eh?" said Aunt Bridget, who seemed now to be wrestling with the fuzzy black pajamas. "Oh, drat this zipper anyway!"

"Then I could do what I want and eat what I want and not have to play the violin and not have to go to school."

"This zipper is not going to work," Aunt Bridget said, not seeming to hear me. "The fuzz keeps getting stuck in the teeth. I am going to have to go with snaps. The really big ones. Whopper poppers they're called. Yes. Whopper poppers are the answer to my dreams, oh my darling gorilla." Aunt Bridget held the gorilla suit and waltzed with it around the apartment. I couldn't help laughing and I felt better. Aunt Bridget stopped for a moment to look at me. "Why don't you go to the park and find Liesl and ask how she likes her life? Maybe it's not as good as it seems."

"Yeah, I could do that," I said, not very enthusiastically. "I met her yesterday. She plays on Gareth's team. I don't think she likes me very much."

"I don't think Liesl likes anyone very much, but I bet she'd be glad to have you talk to her. I think she must be pretty lonely. Go on, give it a try. What's the worst that can happen?"

"She'll scream at me," I said.

"You'll survive," Aunt Bridget said airily. "Meanwhile, I've got to go out and get those whopper poppers."

"How'll I find her?"

"Most likely she'll be by the statue of Colonel Pettingill. She likes to hang out there and draw. Wait till you see her drawings!"

I had three boxes of cereal. Very satisfying. I would have had more, but I could just see my mother's mouth getting wrinkly. *Three* boxes? Oh well, maybe next time I'd get that stuff that tasted like dead hay to make up for this terrible thing I'd done.

Just before going out the door, my violin caught my eye. I took a step toward it. I actually felt like taking it out and playing it. Maybe later when I came back from the park, I'd try it. Maybe Mr. Pettingill would play the violin again and I could sort of pretend to play along.

Out in the park, the piano music was clear and loud. "It's Beethoven," I said to myself, surprised I even knew such a thing, but it was one of the pieces I was learning to play. It was called Ode to Joy. Somehow it made me feel braver about talking to Liesl.

I found her right away, next to the statue of Colonel Pettingill. She was hard to miss. She was wearing the same outfit as the day before, with the tonsil-colored cap on backwards. Her right hand was crammed with chalks and she was crouched over the pavement, her left hand busily drawing. As I came closer, I could see that she was drawing a little girl who was sitting on a bench in front of her.

"Holy cow!" I said. I couldn't believe how good the drawing was.

"There!" said Liesl. She slapped her hands against her skirt, sending chalk dust into the air. "That'll be fifty cents," she said.

"Ooh, that's lovely," said the little girl's mother, handing two quarters to Liesl. "Come see, Janie. It looks just like you, doesn't it, honey?"

"I want it," said the little girl.

"It's on the pavement, you can't have it, honey."

"But I want it," said the little girl.

"When you're twelve years old, come back here and I'll draw your portrait on paper," said Liesl. "If you do what your mother tells you," she added fiercely.

The little girl stared at Liesl and then put her hand in her mother's hand and walked obediently away.

"Fifty cents!" I couldn't keep my eyes off the drawing on the pavement. It looked like a professional had done it. "Is that all you charge? You should charge millions."

"Sometimes I do," said Liesl. She slipped the chalk into the pockets of her apron. "It depends on who I'm drawing for. Or if they want me to draw on paper so they can take it home. Then I make 'em pay through the nose." She looked me up and down. "You're the kid who played first base yesterday, aren't you? Your name is Willy Wilson. Kind of a boring excuse for a name. So what are you doing here? I've never seen you before."

"I'm spending the summer with my aunt Bridget. Bridget McTaggart."

"I know her, she's the costume lady. She puts on plays for the kids in the park sometimes. She's okay, your aunt. She makes me feel regular, like I'm a peanut butter and jelly sandwich instead of something weird that nobody wants, like anchovies or something."

I felt a rush of pride for my aunt, and I thought Liesl might give me a chance now. I stared at her, trying to guess her age. She was small and skinny, but there was a pinched toughness in her face that made her look old. Ages were mixed-up in the park;

Gareth and Liesl seemed old, Aunt Bridget seemed young.

I cleared my throat. "Gareth told me you don't go to school," I said.

I didn't know yet that Liesl was an active volcano. Right away a red blotch flared on her face. A blue vein lit across the bridge of her nose. "What's it to you?" she snapped.

"It's—I hate school," I stammered, nervously backing away from her. "I just think you are so lucky."

"Then you *are* dumb, Willy Wilson, and I don't have time for dumb people." She started to walk away.

A note of music swelled, giving me a bit of courage. "Don't go," I pleaded. "I didn't mean to make you mad."

To my surprise, Liesl stopped and turned. "Want to see a picture of your aunt?" she asked.

I nodded, then sighed. What a moody person she was. Liesl crouched down on the pavement, taking out chalk. She began to draw. I crouched down beside her, not daring to speak, and watched, fascinated, as Liesl's fingers—covered with chalk dust, her nails long and ragged, with half moons of dirt underneath—darted here and there, moving, I was pretty sure, in time to the music. And good grief, she had the biggest hands, the longest fingers, of any kid I had ever seen.

Magically, Aunt Bridget's curly hair and round face began to appear. And then a shadow fell across the drawing and a deep voice called out, "Miss Liesl Summer?"

Liesl and I looked up. A tall red-haired man all in white—he was wearing a white jacket and a white vest and a pair of white trousers—was standing over us.

eight

I never got the education I wanted, and,
you know, I don't think I'll ever get over it.
—*Roland Brookings Jr.*

"Miss Liesl Summer," the man said again.

"You got it," said Liesl. She slapped her hands together and chalk dust rose up in a fine little cloud. She sat back on her heels and stared at the man. "I know you," she said. "You're Roland Brookings, Otto Pettingill's lawyer."

The man set down his briefcase and extended a hand to Liesl. "Roland Brookings *Junior*," he said.

Ignoring him, Liesl sat on the bench the little girl had been sitting on for her portrait. Roland Brookings *Junior* looked like an idiot, standing there with his hand in the air. His fingers were pudgy and freckly, with red hair sprouting on the knuckles, and it looked like he bit his fingernails—not the nail part, but the skin along the edges of the nail. All in all, his hand didn't seem to go with the rest of him, which was smooth and cool and rich-looking.

I stood up, hovering by the bench, feeling anxious. The music suddenly sounded dark. Mr. Brookings pressed a pudgy hand against his nose as if Liesl didn't smell so great (which, to tell the truth, she didn't), and then looked at her with eyes that were two chilly pools of blue.

"I have some news for you from your guardian," he said.

"Spit it out," she said.

"This may come as something of a shock to you," he said slowly.

Liesl shrugged her bony little shoulders. "Out with it," she said.

Mr. Brookings walked over to the bench and sat down next to Liesl, making sure his white suit didn't come too close to her. She moved away from him, too, scrunching herself into a little ball, holding her arms tightly around her bony knees.

"Come on, Roland Brookings Junior, out with it," she said again, glaring at him with flinty eyes. "What's going to happen to me? Is my stupid guardian going to stick me in an orphanage or what?"

"Stupid, is he?" Mr. Brookings said indignantly. "He gives you a healthy annual income, my dear, pays for your large apartment in an expensive part of town." He stopped, maybe remembering that he was supposed to be nice. "Liesl, I'm here to tell you that you are to live with a family now."

Even Liesl was speechless for a moment. She uncurled and sat up. "A family?"

Mr. Brookings made funny noises in his throat. I figured he was nervous, because whenever my math teacher called on me at school, I got nervous, and being nervous made me clear my throat a lot.

"A couple, actually," said Mr. Brookings.

"A couple of families?" Liesl asked. "There have to be that many people to take care of me?"

"I mean a couple," said Mr. Brookings. "A man and a woman. They don't have children of their own, so when they heard that Mr. Pettingill was looking for a home for you—"

"Why is Mr. Pettingill looking for a home for me and how come he isn't here to tell me so himself?" Liesl got up off the bench and began to pace back and forth in front of it. "He's such a slimy, jerky creep and if I ever see him again I'll spit in his face." She turned to Mr. Brookings. "And you can tell him that."

Mr. Brookings slumped slightly and groaned and ran a pudgy, freckly hand across his face. "Delightful child," he said. Then he sat up straighter. "Listen. My dear, I am Otto Pettingill's attorney. He sent me here to inform you of his intentions." Then he muttered, "What am I but his servant," probably not realizing that I was standing just behind him and could hear him clearly. Like most grown-ups, he didn't seem to notice me anyway. "He is not able to be here, so it is my duty to carry out his wishes," he said, suddenly becoming businesslike. Looking at his watch, he stood up and picked up his briefcase.

"I will be bringing Mr. and Mrs. Dolittle to meet you here at noon," he said. "Right here beside the statue. Can you remember that?"

"That's in only two hours," I blurted out, looking at my watch. I couldn't help it—I didn't want Liesl to disappear the moment I met her. Mr. Brookings glanced at me, surprised to see me there. "Yes," he said.

"I won't go," said Liesl. Her face was blazing with red patches. "And you can't make me. Why should I?"

Mr. Brookings' face turned red, too. With his red hair and red face on top of his white suit, he looked like a match flaring up, except for his blue eyes, which seemed like fire without warmth.

"Why? Why should you? Because you can go to school now, my dear," he said, his knuckles white from strangling the handle of his briefcase. "The Dolittles have a connection with the East Park Day School, a very nice, small private school that is willing to take on a girl who has had no formal schooling whatsoever. There are not many schools that would do this. It may be your best hope of going to any school at all."

Liesl's face turned very white and the vein across the bridge of her nose looked like a blue gash. "School," she whispered. "School. Do you hear that, Willy Wilson? I can go to school!"

Mr. Brookings smiled a huge crocodile smile and

seemed to relax. "I presume this means we shall be seeing you at noon," he said.

"You bet," said Liesl.

"Fabulous," said Mr. Brookings. He bowed slightly to Liesl and walked away.

Fabulous. I hated the way he said that. He sounded so fake and phony. *Fabulous.* Through his teeth and through his nose.

"I'll get to wash blackboards and clap erasers and help the teacher take attendance," Liesl cried joyfully. "I'll get to jump rope at recess and play hopscotch." She jumped on the pavement, twirling an imaginary jump rope. "Teddy bear, teddy bear, turn around," she chanted. "Teddy bear, teddy bear, touch the ground. Teddy bear, teddy bear, tie your shoe. Teddy bear, teddy bear, now skiddoo."

Liesl stopped, looking pleased with herself. "Isn't that great, Willy Wilson?"

I took a deep breath. All I could think of was that she was in for a big disappointment. "Who told you that school would be like that?" I asked.

"Mitch Bloom," she said. "He told me that rhyme only one time and I remembered it. And he told me about clapping erasers."

"Sit down for a minute and let me tell you a few things," I said, in charge for once in my life. If there was anything I knew about, it was school. Liesl sat down on the bench, her face open and shiny, not ready at all to take in the bad stuff I was going to tell her. "School isn't just recess and games," I said. "They make you do homework and take tests and they're always making you learn boring things. The teachers yell at you for stupid things. Sometimes the kids are really mean and they gang up on you and they're sure to gang up on you because . . . because . . ."

"Because why, Willy Wilson?" The vein between Liesl's eyes throbbed dangerously and her face was becoming blotchy again like the underside of one of Mom's goldfish. "Because I'm a *weirdo,* is that what you're trying to say?"

"What about the Dolittles?" I managed to blurt out. "That family you're going to go live with?"

"What about them?"

"You don't know anything about them." I cleared my throat and pushed on. "They'll be all over you, telling you what to do every minute. You'll have to brush your hair, and your . . . teeth." I muttered that last word, *teeth.* I had a fairly good idea Liesl didn't brush her teeth on a regular basis.

"So what do you care, anyhow, Willy Wilson? What are you getting so bent out of shape for? You act like this is happening to you."

I took another deep breath and stared at Liesl. She sat on the bench, her scrawny legs swinging away, squinting back at me. "I don't know," I said, cramming my fists into my pockets. The truth was, I liked her life. Yeah, that was it. I liked her freedom. She was going to have to give up the right not to brush her teeth, and I bet *she* didn't have to make her bed every morning of her life. "Don't you even wonder why Mr. Pettingill isn't going to be your guardian anymore?"

"No!" She scrambled off the bench and, crouching on the pavement again, took a fistful of chalks from an apron pocket. Her hand darted here and there. A head appeared—a bald head with a big nose and a pointy beard. "There's Otto Pettingill," she said, and then she spat. A great splotch of saliva landed on the nose. She smeared the picture with the toe of a holey red sneaker. "That's what I think of him."

I could feel my breakfast cereal rising in my stomach. "But I'd do anything to live the way you do," I said.

"Since he's getting rid of me, why don't you go find Uncle Otto and apply for the position?"

"You think he really could . . . adopt me?" The piano sounded a series of chords right at that moment. They made me think of marble stairs leading to a palace where Otto Pettingill was sitting on a throne with light shining all around him.

"I think Otto Pettingill can do anything he wants to," said Liesl. "He's like the king around here. But your parents wouldn't let you be adopted by someone else."

"I don't see why not," I said. "Then my dad could get someone who doesn't get on his nerves the way I do."

"How could you get on anyone's nerves?" Liesl asked scornfully. "You're such a wimp you couldn't get on a piece of spaghetti's nerves."

"Yeah, but I do," I said, suddenly proud. "You should see my dad when I can't remember something, like how many times nine goes into fifty-six. He digs his fingers into his eyes and he pulls on his top lip like this." I imitated my father and Liesl laughed.

"I bet you don't make him mad the way Belle Vera makes me mad, though."

"Who is Belle Vera?"

"The lady I have to live with. She's too nice. She feeds whole-wheat crumbs to the birds so they'll be healthy—that's the kind of person *she* is. But speaking of the devil, I see her coming. Come on, let's get out of here. She probably found out about Otto Pettingill giving me away and she's going to make a big deal out of it." She scrambled up and grabbed my arm and began pulling me along. "Come on," she said again. "We'll go to Mitch Bloom's and hide out."

nine

When my wife left me,
I thought I had lost everything.
Then I realized I had a tree.

—*Mitch Bloom*

Liesl pulled me into the woods where bicycle and jogging paths wound through the trees. Here the city noises were muffled, but the piano was still sweet and clear. The park trees were tall and thick, and because of the music, I thought, their branches curved in the air like the arms of ballet dancers.

As I chased after Liesl, part of me was thinking about the trees and part of me was noticing how bad her posture was, how she slouched as she ran, and part of me was thinking about Roland Brookings and his icy blue eyes. I just didn't think he was up to any good. Maybe I'd try one more time to make Liesl listen to me.

"Liesl!" I called out. "Liesl, wait up!" She turned around. "I don't think you should go."

"Why not?" she asked. "I always go to Mitch Bloom's."

"I don't mean to Mitch Bloom's. I mean to the Dolittles'. Those people you're supposed to live with."

Liesl took a step toward me. "You just want me to rot and die, don't you?" she said, her face turning crimson. "Why don't you just crawl back into whatever hole you came out of and leave me alone?" She jammed her hands into her apron pockets and spun back into forward march position.

I should have turned around right then and there and left her, but I was attached to her in some weird way. I felt as if I had to stay with her until she met up with those Dolittles.

Liesl stopped suddenly in front of a large oak, the tallest and widest tree in the woods. "Here we are," she said. She turned and grinned as if she'd never been mad at me a moment in her life, and I was too distracted by what I was looking at to care. Behind the tree was a field blazing with color. There seemed to be millions of flowers, orange and red, yellow and blue; and at the far end of the field was a greenhouse.

"Mitch Bloom's flowers," Liesl said proudly. "Okay, now let's go up."

She put two dirty fingers up to the trunk of the tree and opened a little door in the bark. Inside were two switches mounted in a gray box. She flicked the bottom switch, and I heard a grinding motor sound coming from the top of the tree. I suddenly noticed two steel rods running down the whole length of the tree. Traveling down those rods was a large wooden box. The ground beneath my feet was vibrating.

"Holy cow!" I said. "What is it?"

"Mitch Bloom's elevator," Liesl said matter-of-factly.

"Holy cow," I said again. "He lives up there?" By craning my neck, I could just make out a structure high up in the branches.

"Yeah, what did you think?"

By this time the elevator had reached us. Liesl opened the door and said, "On tray, silver plate."

"What?" I asked, wondering if Liesl were muttering a magic spell that would make the elevator go up, but then she shut the door and flicked a switch from a box identical to the one that had been on the tree. I felt the elevator lift up off the ground. The walls were made of plywood and they kind of shivered; I didn't feel good at all.

"*On tray, silver plate* is French. Belle Vera is French, you know. It makes me sound educated to speak French, don't you think? Like I really will be when I go to that school. The East Park Day School is a very fine school; the kids wear blazers."

"Are you sure this elevator is safe?" I asked, ignoring her dumb remark about blazers. I had to wear a blazer at my school, too, every Monday, and it didn't mean it was a very fine school.

"Course it's safe. Mitch Bloom built it."

There was a buzzing and the elevator stopped. Liesl opened the door. Standing right by the door was Mitch Bloom, the tall thin man I had seen the day before at the flower stand. "Hey, my little flower," he said, bending down to kiss Liesl's cheek. "I am always glad to see you, but please, next time give me a buzz down below before you come up. I like to know who's advancing on me."

I hung back, hardly able to believe my eyes. I was looking at a living room that could have been a living room anywhere—there was a couch, an easy chair, a desk and chair, pictures on the walls—except that when you looked out the windows, you could see the branches and leaves of the oak tree, and in the spaces between them, far below, all the colors in the field of flowers.

"And who's your friend? Where are your manners, Liesl? I'm Mitch," he said, putting out a hand.

"That's Willy Wilson, he thinks I'm a weirdo." Liesl laughed. I think it was the first time I had actually heard her laugh. She was hanging on Mitch's arm, looking less pinched than usual.

"Willy Wilson," said Mitch. His big Adam's apple bobbed. "Now I remember. I saw you with Gareth yesterday morning, didn't I? New to the park?"

"He's staying with Bridget McTaggart, the costume lady, and he plays first base for our team."

Our team. So that's how she thought of it—she *did* care about it. I'd have to remember to tell Gareth. And she said I played first base, so casually, as if I'd been playing for the team for years; and she didn't seem mad or disgusted about it, either.

"Ha!" said Mitch, clapping a hand on my shoulder. "Well, Willy Wilson, welcome to Gill Park! First baseman, eh? A valuable position. Gareth's been looking for a first baseman for ages. He must be as happy as a sunflower in manure."

"I never called you a weirdo," I said, turning to Liesl.

"You thought it, Willy Wilson. I saw you thinking it when you met the team. You were thinking it when you told me about school, how the kids are going to beat me up."

"I didn't—" I started to say, but Mitch was already speaking.

"A fine lady, your aunt," he was saying. "Tragedy about that husband of hers—a talented man. But she's talented, too, and young and beautiful. She'll find her way."

"Can I look around?" I asked.

"Be my guest," said Mitch, opening another door at the far end of the living room.

"Holy cow!" I said again. Before me was a tiny kitchen. There was a black stove with a pipe going up through the roof. "That's what you cook on?"

"Yup, you bet," said Mitch, eyeing his stove proudly. "My stove, she warms me, she warms my soup, she warms my socks." He pointed to a rack above the stove where a row of socks was hanging up to dry. "All at once. Very economical. And here's where I sleep."

Mitch opened another door. The room was tiny, completely filled with a bed. "My *bed* room," he said, chuckling. His Adam's apple bobbed like a yo-yo. "And my *bath* room." He pointed to another room. In it was a toilet and a bathtub with lion's feet. "Found that at a tag sale. I was a proud man the day I hauled that tub up here, but Mabel, she didn't care for it."

"Mabel's his no-good wife who ran off and left him," said Liesl as we walked back into the living room.

"Yeah," said Mitch with a heavy sigh. "Some plants, you dig 'em up and plant 'em in a different place, they'll take to that new soil. Well, Mabel, she didn't. She kind of up and wilted." Mitch rubbed a hand over his bouncy gray hair. It probably felt good to do that. If I'd had his kind of hair, I'd have done that a lot. "But, see, she left, and then the next day, what do you think happened? Guess who turned up on my doorstep—I mean, at my tree trunk? Well, this little flower right here. Now how about a strawberry shake? Come here and help me cut up strawberries, Liesl."

I sat and looked out a window at a squirrel that was sleeping on a branch and thought that Liesl wasn't really flowerlike; if anything, she was a weed or one of those dangerous jungle things that leaps out and strangles you. Definitely not your everyday peanut butter and jelly sandwich. Except now, working beside Mitch, frowning as she concentrated on cutting the strawberries, she did look almost regular.

"Can you read to me now, Mitch Bloom?" she asked when they had finished. "Mitch Bloom is reading to me from a book called *Swiss Family Robinson*."

"It's my favorite book on account of the family lives in a tree house," he said.

They settled together on the couch and I sat opposite in a chair and listened while Mitch read. It was a pretty good book, and Mitch read it really well. I was surprised that Liesl had the patience to sit and listen, but she didn't move a muscle through any of it, even though Mitch read for a long time.

"Okay, my little flower," he said finally. "I think my voice needs a rest." He got up and poured himself some more strawberry drink.

"Guess what, Mitch Bloom, I get to go to school," Liesl suddenly burst out. I was wondering when she was going to get around to telling him.

Mitch put down his glass and stared at her. "You get to go to school? What kind of school?"

"The East Park Day School."

Mitch looked puzzled. "How is that?"

Liesl finally looked up. "I'm being adopted."

"You're being adopted?" He frowned. "I'm—I'm sorry to hear that. I was actually hoping to do that myself."

Liesl leaped up from the couch. "You *were*?"

Mitch nodded. "I have been thinking about writing a letter to Mr. Pettingill. I've even been drawing up some plans for enlarging the old house."

Before Liesl could say anything, there was a buzzing from a box by the elevator door. Mitch jumped and said, "Someone wants to come up." He went over and pressed a button on the box and a deep woman's voice with a thick accent came through it. "It's Belle, Mitch, may I ascend?"

"You bet," said Mitch.

"Oh, kafooie," Liesl muttered. She looked longingly at a window, as if she wanted to escape through it.

ten

The English language,
she taste like the cold soup of the tomatoes;
the French language,
she taste like a warm soup with the tomatoes,
the potato, the green beans, the onion,
and, ma chérie, with the garlic!

—Belle Vera

Mitch flicked a switch and the room shook slightly as the elevator box shimmied down the rods to the ground to pick up Belle Vera.

The elevator finally came back up and the door opened and a large woman umphed her way out of it. "Ah, such a shame!" she exclaimed as she stepped into the room. Her hair was gray and curly, her face rosy and plump, and the rest of her was plump, too. She made me think of a large pigeon. She seemed so friendly and safe; I figured Liesl was probably the only person in the world without the sense to like her. "This is a cat-a-strophe! The worst day of my life! Worse than when I was retired by the school!" she said, the words heaving out of her mouth.

"Come here, Belle; come sit down. Is this true, that Liesl is being adopted?"

Belle Vera plopped herself down on Mitch's couch. "That lift of yours, Mitch. It is a trap of death, if you ask me. If it wasn't the worst day of my life, you wouldn't have caught me dead in it. Ah ha, ha, that's droll, isn't it?"

"A bit of irony, yes," said Mitch, nodding. "But what is happening, Belle, this worst day of your life? Has it to do with what Liesl has been telling me? She is to be adopted?"

"I am, I am!" Liesl blurted out.

Mitch raised his eyebrows at Belle Vera. "Is this really so?"

Belle plumped her hands on her knees. "That species of beast, that Otto Pettingill, he has no consideration for the feelings of people. Here these many years have I been taking care of this child and oh la la! All of the sudden he sends that advocate of his around to me. Crisp like a cucumber, that man says, 'We will no longer be requiring your services, Madame Vera.' I mean, Monsieur P., he never considers him how I feel after all these years. Me, I would like to tell that species of ancient dust just what I think of him." She stopped speaking for a moment and crossed her arms and looked as if she were *thinking* just what she thought of him. "I remember me the day that advocate first came to me, it was the day after they retired me from the school. I was so *triste,* so sad, so in grief, for I loved the school so much. 'You are getting too old, Madame,' they said to me. In France, the old age is respected, *non*? But the advocate, he say to me, 'She is to have no influence from the outside. No television, no film, no school.' Oh la la! I happen to know she has spent half her days in the magazines watching TV."

"When she says *magazines* she means stores," Liesl said scornfully. I bit my lip, not understanding why Liesl was so mean to Belle.

"They say to me, 'The little girl is to be a child of nature,'" Belle went on, "'Just to make sure she does not get hurt and see that the basic needs are taken care of.' The basic needs!" She snorted. "What does that mean? Is not the love a basic need? Is not the love, the tenderness, and, oh yes, the discipline, a basic need? Was I not a *professeur* for forty year and do I not know some little thing about the heart and mind and life of the child? Oh la la!" She shook her head. "Just look at her!"

We all looked at Liesl. She was sitting on the floor, curled up at Mitch's feet.

"Well, I can say this," said Mitch. He took one of Liesl's hands in his. "She has the most beautiful and strong hands of any child I've ever seen."

I thought Liesl would be pleased but she stood up and started screaming. "Oh my God!" she yelled. "What time is it?"

"It's almost twelve," said Mitch.

"Oh my God!" she yelled again. "I have to go."

She ran toward the elevator and swung open the door.

"Hold on," said Mitch. "We're all coming."

"Oh God, I'll be so late."

Mitch helped Belle Vera up from the couch, and as Belle slowly stepped into the elevator, Liesl was practically jumping out of her skin with impatience. "I'm gonna miss them, I know it. I'm gonna miss them, and my chance to go to school."

Mitch stepped into the elevator next to her and put a hand on her shoulder. "Shut the door, will you please, Willy?" he asked calmly. With his other hand he flicked the switch to send us down. "Listen to me, Liesl," he said. "They'll wait for you; believe me, they will."

The elevator shivered and shook all the way down. I couldn't help wondering if it would hold all our weight. As soon as we stopped moving, Liesl dashed out the door and raced ahead of us through the woods. I felt sorry for Belle Vera, who was puffing and panting, walking as fast as she could. "You stay with her," Mitch said to me, nodding at Belle, "and I'll go on ahead with Liesl."

I forced myself to keep pace with the plump old woman. "Thank you, my friend," she said to me. "You are so amicable, and I don't even know your name."

"I'm Willy Wilson," I said. "I'm staying with my aunt, Bridget McTaggart. She makes costumes—" I started to say.

"Oh, Brigitte, but of course!" Belle exclaimed, smiling. I smiled, too. Everyone seemed to know my aunt. "She made Liesl's apron, you know. Her apron of chalk. And what will happen to the child's drawing now?"

We finally reached the statue where Mr. Brookings had told Liesl to meet him. And there he was, still in his white outfit, and beside him were a man and a woman. Liesl and Mitch Bloom stood facing them.

"O mon dieu," said Belle, stopping for a moment and putting her hand against her heart. "I don't know if I can support this, Vill-ee. My heart, she is not so good, and I think it breaks. Nobody knows the child as I do; she acts like the tough little bird, but inside she is only broken, do you see?" She took my arm. "You help me, please, Vill-ee; I have to see what these persons who adopt her are like, but I cannot do it alone."

Mr. and Mrs. Dolittle were wearing matching light blue T-shirts and khaki pants. They were very clean. Their hair was very combed. Mrs. Dolittle was holding a balloon that was in the shape of Winnie-the-Pooh. As we approached, Mr. Brookings was saying, "You couldn't have ended up with nicer, warmer people, Liesl."

"You see, Liesl," Mr. Dolittle said, tilting his head and smiling and showing off a lot of white teeth, "Rebecca and I don't have children of our own." He reached out and gave Liesl's hand a little squeeze.

"So we know you'll come to be our own special, beautiful little girl," said Mrs. Dolittle. I could smell her perfume. She had a lot of it on. She bent down and peered into Liesl's face. "Would you like that, sweetie?" She took Liesl's other hand.

Liesl's face was very pale. The vein across the bridge of her nose was very blue. She took a deep breath and nodded, but at the same time pulled her hands away from the Dolittles' hands and stuffed them into the pockets of her apron.

Belle bustled forward. "Me, I am Madame Belle Vera," she said. The Dolittles looked at her blankly. "The curd of the cheese, he has not told you," she muttered, nodding at Mr. Brookings. "Me, I have been her *gouvernante* all these years. I just thought—" Poor Belle couldn't go on. Her face crumpled and the tears began to slide down her face. She plunged her hand into the pocket of her dress and took out a handkerchief. "I've gotten to know this child, is all." She sniffed. "I'm used to her ways, and I just thought if you were looking for someone to help out—"

"Oh," said Mrs. Dolittle with a little laugh. "All those years of being a forlorn little waif are over for Liesl forever. She'll have all the best. We won't be needing your help now, thank you very much, Madame."

Belle took a step back, and it was a good thing the bench was right there. She collapsed onto it.

"I can't see any reason why we can't begin our new life together right now, can you?" Mr. Dolittle asked brightly.

One of Liesl's hands uncurled out of a pocket. She brought out a piece of purple chalk. It wavered in the air. "Can I draw at your house?" she asked in a high, thin voice.

"Draw? Of course you can draw," said Mrs. Dolittle. "But you'll never have to get yourself dirty drawing on a sidewalk again. You'll have nice paints and all the paper and canvas you could wish for. And Liesl!" She gave a little skip of excitement. "We have so much to do before school. We'll go shopping for clothes and get you looking so smart! It'll be such fun!" Then she tied the string of the balloon around Liesl's wrist. "Here's Winnie-the-Pooh for you, dear. You like Winnie-the-Pooh, don't you?" Liesl shrugged and Mrs. Dolittle said, "You don't know Winnie-the-Pooh? Oh, we *do* have some catching up to do!"

"Off you go then with your new little family," said Mr. Brookings cheerfully.

"Thank you so much for everything, Mr. Brookings," said Mrs. Dolittle.

"It's been a real pleasure working with you," said Mr. Dolittle, reaching forward to shake Mr. Brookings' hand.

"The pleasure's been all mine," said Mr. Brookings. "And it's *fabulous* to see the child in such good hands."

"Hey, Willy Wilson," Liesl said, yanking the apron off her waist. She clumped it in a bunch, chalks and all, and pushed it into my hands. "Hold these for me, will ya?"

Then each Dolittle took one of her arms and held her between them as if she were a little kid who couldn't walk yet. The Winnie-the-Pooh balloon floated behind their heads, hanging back, as if reluctant to go with them.

"Well, that's that," said Mr. Brookings, picking up his briefcase. "Good day to you all." He nodded to us and then walked briskly away.

Soon, Mr. Brookings, Liesl, and the Dolittles were nothing but backs blurring into the distance.

"Well!" said Belle Vera. Her face was red and the tears were pouring down her cheeks. "Not even a *merci beaucoup* for all your hard work over the years. Not even, 'I am sure you'll miss the little girl a great deal in spite of all her terrible ways.' It is not her fault, *la pauvre petite*." Belle began to sob. "Oh, I shall never see her again!"

Mitch Bloom, on the other hand, was laughing. It had started as a sort of chuckle, and now he was bellowing, slapping his knee. I couldn't believe it.

Belle Vera stopped her sobbing and turned to stare at him. "What on the earth?" she gasped. "Have you gone mad?"

"Hang on to that apron of chalk, Willy Wilson," said Mitch. "She won't last more than one day with that lot." He roared with laughter again. "It'll be a toss-up. Who'll quit first, them or her?"

I couldn't help smiling, and I held the apron carefully so that the chalk wouldn't spill out.

"Hey, Wilson! Where've you been? We have to practice today, wicked bad—come on!" Gareth was standing in front of me, waving his glove in my face. "Willy, hello, did you hear me?"

I heard Gareth all right, but I heard something else, too. I heard the leaves in the trees rustling, the shouting of little kids who were playing nearby . . . the engines of cars, the panting of a dog that sat in the sun two feet away. A jogger passed and I could hear his sneakers squeaking. I thought for a moment that I could hear everything, even the sounds of the branches stretching up to the sky and the roots of the trees digging a little deeper.

"Willy?" Everyone was staring at me—Belle Vera, Mitch Bloom, Gareth Pugh.

"The music stopped," I said. "Otto Pettingill's not playing the music."

"Oh," said Mitch. He cocked his head like a dog, listening, and then shrugged. "He's just taking a break, that's all. He can't play all the time. Come on, Belle, let's get you home. And boys, we'll be seeing you later." Mitch helped Belle Vera to her feet, and then the two of them walked slowly away.

eleven

I had a vision—to create a park at whose center
would be a fountain that spurted
plumes of colors, in a rhythm
that would match a Mozart sonata.

—*Otto Pettingill*

"Come on, Willy, let's go," said Gareth. "And where's Liesl? We better drag her along. She'll never remember on her own."

"Liesl won't be coming today," I said.

"What?" Gareth's freckles bounced.

"She's been adopted," I said. "Just now. She's going to go live with a family."

"No!" Gareth cried out as if he had been punched in the stomach. He dropped his glove and tore off his cap and twisted it in agony. "She can't do that. She's my third baseman. We're playing the Sharks some-time next week."

I stared at Gareth in amazement. Didn't it matter to him that she had been adopted, or was baseball all he cared about? "She might still play on the team," I said. "She seems real proud of it."

Gareth slowly put his cap back on and picked up his glove. "Yeah, well, we'll see. We might as well go to practice. There isn't anything we can do about it anyway."

I dragged along after Gareth. Everything about the park suddenly seemed wrong: I noticed litter and broken glass and cigarette butts mixed in with the barky stuff they put in the flower beds, and the flower beds weren't even that well weeded and a lot of the leaves were bug-eaten. Half the paint was peeling off a bench, so it looked like it had a horrible skin disease. Another bench was all scarred up with people's names and dumb things like "Kara loves Jason."

I passed a group of older kids hanging out, look-ing edgy and uncomfortable with each other. A girl dressed completely in pink was talking on a cell phone and crying, while a guy who wasn't wearing a shirt was trying to do tricks on a bike right in front of her. He wasn't paying any attention to the fact that she was upset. He had a tattoo of a big spider on his arm and he was wearing army pants and black boots.

Capasso, Hoscowitz, Dixon, Toenail, the others—they were all there on the baseball diamond. Gareth told them about Liesl, how she might not be on the team anymore. Not one of them seemed too sad about it—and I can't say I blamed them. And then Gareth lined us up for batting. I never could hit the ball and today wasn't any different. I'd swing, too early, too late. I wanted the music back. I felt heavy and my head was filled with sand. The truth was, we were all so bad that Gareth didn't even bother to yell. He pitched at us with a pinched face without saying a word. It was almost worse than when he did yell.

"Let's call it quits," he finally said. "I'll see you guys tomorrow. You go home and think about what you want. Think if you really want to play ball and come back here with a decision." He crammed his hands into his pockets and stalked away.

"Is he crying?" Capasso asked in disbelief.

"He's just sweatin' mad," I said, coming to Gareth's defense.

We all looked at each other and shrugged.

"He's being a little overdramatic," Dixon said. "It's not like we *have* to be doing this."

"One bad day and he pops," said Toenail.

"You have to admit, we were pretty bad," I said. I didn't want the guys to quit on Gareth today of all days. First Liesl, and then the music—I really didn't want to lose the only baseball team I'd been happy to play on. "And he's worried about our game."

"It's just a *game*," said Toenail.

"Well, you gotta care about *some*thing," I said. "It might as well be a game. I mean, some people care about their hair color, you know?"

The guys laughed, even Toenail. He reached over and punched me in a friendly way. "Hey, you're a funny dude. At least we don't have to deal with that freak of a girl anymore."

"Yeah, what a relief. Hey, see ya guys tomorrow," said Hoscowitz. "We're gonna kill those Sharks when we do play 'em."

Everyone said, "Yeah," or grunted, or something to show they agreed and then they all drifted away. I drifted off, too, thinking that it would be great to go back to the apartment and see Aunt Bridget. She, at least, would be cheerful.

I was wrong about that. When I went up the stairs and opened the door, I found her sitting at the sewing table with her head in the black fuzz, her face all wet and blotchy from crying.

"Oh boy," she said, sitting up as I came in. "You caught me in a Roger moment—sorry about that, Willy." In among the fuzz was a picture of Uncle Roger. She picked it up and wiped some hairs off it. "Lately this photograph is practically the only way I can remember how he looked, except sometimes at night, when I can see his face floating above my head in the dark." She sniffed and laughed. "That sounds spooky, doesn't it? But bit by bit I feel as if I'm losing him, the way water slowly goes down the drain. The only thing that really helps is the park music. Like if Otto plays a Mozart sonata, then I can picture Roger perfectly, like what he was wearing the last time Otto played that piece, you know. I can see him washing the car, or the walk we took around the neighborhood, or him fixing the flat on his ridiculous ancient bike. He never would get rid of that bike. Or I can see the shirt he was wearing and how his blue eyes filled up with laughter. It's like a time machine, that music. It can help me remember a whole day we had together all over again. So today wasn't a good day for old Otto to decide not to play, but I guess he has to take a break sometime." She shook the hair out of her eyes and pushed back her chair and stood up. "Sorry, Willy, I don't get like this very often."

"It's okay, I don't mind," I said. I felt honored that Aunt Bridget wouldn't try to hide her feelings from me the way I knew my parents would have.

She seemed to read my mind. "I know your dad would never get all weepy like this. Stiff upper lip and all that." I smiled. Aunt Bridget really was very good at imitating my father. "But I've finished three suits, Willy. Only twenty-seven to go."

"Who is it who wants thirty gorilla suits, anyway?" I asked.

"It's the Palace, the comedy club in town. Apparently they're doing a Rockette-style dance of gorillas. We humans always seem to find gorillas so funny. I guess because we're so much alike. Now, Willy, tell me about your day. Less gloomy than mine, I hope. Did you have a chance to talk to Liesl?"

"A really weird thing happened," I said. "I was talking to her and this guy came over. He's Otto Pettingill's lawyer, I guess, and he told Liesl that Mr. Pettingill said she was going to be adopted by these people called the Dolittles, and that she'd get to go to school, and she was all excited because she wants to go to school, and a little later we went and met the people who adopted her and she went off with them."

"Really?" Aunt Bridget put Uncle Roger's photograph back on the bureau, where it had been before, and sat down at the table again and stared at me with interest. One of the best things about Aunt Bridget, I thought, was how she really listened. It made it so much easier for me to talk.

"She was so excited about getting to go to school, I don't think she was thinking about what kind of people would adopt her or anything. Oh, and Belle Vera, who has always taken care of her, was all upset, but Liesl didn't seem to care, and I don't even think she liked Belle Vera that much but I don't see why."

Aunt Bridget shook her head and clicked her tongue against her teeth. "Poor Belle. She really is a saint to have put up with that child for as long as she has."

"Why does Liesl treat Belle Vera like that? She seems so nice."

Aunt Bridget shook her head again. "Liesl's a wild child. She doesn't know what's nice and not nice."

"Also, before she went off with the Dolittles, we went up into Mitch Bloom's house."

Aunt Bridget smiled. "You went up into Mitch's tree house? How lucky you are! Isn't it amazing?"

I nodded. "It is amazing! It's so cool. I didn't think anyone could live like that."

"But back to Liesl. Tell me about the Dolittles. What were they like?"

"They seemed . . . well, clean . . ." It was the only adjective I could think of. "They seemed excited about adopting her because they don't have any kids, but they don't really seem . . . her type, I guess."

Aunt Bridget laughed and said, "Honestly, Willy, I'm not sure who *would* be her type. But what a nice thing to have happen to her. I hope it goes well."

Off and on for the rest of the day, I thought about Liesl and wondered how she was doing. Every little sound seemed to put me on edge, mostly because Mr. Pettingill still wasn't playing the music.

At one point I took out my violin thinking I would make my own music, and then I decided it was too much work to tune it. Maybe if I were great at playing it would be worth the trouble, but I'd just saw away and screech and squeak and make myself feel worse.

Aunt Bridget wasn't her usual cheerful self either. At about nine o'clock that night she said, "I'm going to bed, Willy. My energy for gorillas is not, alas, with me today. Tomorrow a new day will dawn and all will be well."

But when the next day dawned, and Aunt Bridget and I were sitting at the breakfast table, there was a pounding on the door, and both Aunt Bridget and I said, "Gareth," at the same moment, and sure enough, in he exploded, waving a newspaper in our faces.

"Watch out, Gareth, take it easy," said Aunt Bridget as he almost knocked over her glass of orange juice.

"Look at this!" He shoved the paper under her nose. "They're turning the park into a shopping mall."

"What?" Aunt Bridget took the paper from Gareth and slowly began to read. "'Pettingill offers Gill Park to highest bidder. Otto Pettingill, through his attorney, Roland N. Brookings Jr., has announced his intention to offer the parkland to the highest bidder. Response has been immediate. Frank Featherstone, of Featherstone Associates, Inc., is proposing to buy the park and has already outlined plans for a new shopping mall. Mr. Brookings said that Mr. Pettingill is not available for comment.'"

Gareth looked at her wildly. "What are we going to do? How can I manage a team if there's no place to play baseball?"

Aunt Bridget was standing now, the paper still in her hand. She walked slowly over to an open window that looked out onto the park. "How can you manage a baseball team, Gareth, and how can Mitch Bloom live in his tree house, and how can the fountain send up its plumes of color at night, and how can I—" She couldn't finish the sentence. I went and stood beside her.

The room filled with the sound of passing cars, and then of loud laughter as two people directly below us seemed almost to fall over about something funny, and then we could hear a crying baby, and then a truck pulled over and there was a great clatter as it opened its back doors and rolled out a ramp, and somewhere farther down the street there was a kind of rolling rumbling as a kid went by on a skateboard—

"It's bald out there," said Aunt Bridget. "It's naked. Without the music—" She sighed. "It's raw. Excuse me, boys. I'm just going to go for a short walk. I need to get some air."

twelve

When I was born, I was as fresh as new green leaves,
and when I was five, I was glad with the greenness of all things,
and when I was ten, a new anxiety was born; how green I felt—
and when I was fifteen, girls turned me green,
and when I was twenty, green dollars burned in my pocket,
and when I was twenty-five, the world seemed to
    enlarge before me, a green expanse . . .
and now I am thirty, I catch a glimpse of faraway green pastures—
But I am not sure yet what other greenness awaits me.

—*Jerry Rabinowitz*

Gareth and I looked at each other. I felt completely, stinking horrible. I was really mad at Otto Pettingill for doing this, for making Aunt Bridget so miserable, for dumping Liesl, for wrecking Gareth's baseball career. Mitch Bloom wouldn't have a place to live, Old Violet wouldn't have a bench to sit on—all for what? A mall. A *mall,* for Pete's sake!

"So we have to find him," I said.

"Find . . . him?"

"Otto Pettingill," I said. "And ask him not to sell the park and tell him to start playing the music again. He can't quit just like that without any warning." I was starting to yell. "The music is how she remembers Uncle Roger! He can't—"

Gareth was standing beside me now. His mouth was open and I could see the rubber bands quivering inside his mouth. "Oh sure, Willy," he said, laughing slightly. "You're just going to go up to his apartment and knock on his door."

"Yes, I am," I said.

"And then he'll come to his door and say, 'Oh, Willy, how do you do? So glad to see you. I've been hoping you'd come to see me.'"

"Maybe he will," I said.

"Well, why not?" Gareth said slowly. "At least we can find out why he's doing this." He took off his cap, punched it, and then jammed it back on his head. "I'm with you, pal. Let's go."

"Now?" I asked, taken by surprise.

"No time like the present," he said.

We went down the stairs and out to the park. I didn't feel zapped as I stepped into it. Not taller or stronger or zippier or any of the rest of it. Aunt Bridget was right. The park did feel bald or naked or raw without the music.

We walked by Mitch's flower stand and there he was, a newspaper spread out on the counter before him. "You see this, boys?" He jabbed at the newspaper with a pair of shears. "Shopping mall! Sheesh.

They put plastic lilacs in those places. How could he even think of such a thing?"

"What do you think is going on, Mitch?" Gareth asked. "Why do you think he's selling the park?"

"Beats me, kid," said Mitch. "But guess what?" He reached beneath his counter and brought up a stack of paper. "We're going to protest. Petitions, boys."

I picked one up and read it: "'We the undersigned do formally protest the taking of Gill Park from the People and the Destruction of the Land for Purposes of Commercial Enterprise.'" Underneath were lines for people to sign their names on.

"So you take a bunch of these, boys, and you take 'em around and get people to sign 'em."

"Do you really think this will help?" Gareth asked.

"Gotta do something," said Mitch.

Gareth and I walked away with petitions.

"I mean, if Otto Pettingill wants to sell his park, we're not going to stop him," said Gareth.

"Yeah," I said. "But it's where Mitch lives. He can't just sit there and let it happen."

"Yeah, you're right," said Gareth.

"So where does Otto Pettingill live?" I asked.

"Thirteen East Park," said Gareth.

When we got to Thirteen East Park, there was a jumble of vans and cars and trucks and people swarming all over the place. "Yikes," said Gareth. "Every TV and radio and newspaper reporter in the city of Gloria is here. And every policeman. We're not even going to get one toe into the lobby."

We stood on the sidewalk, staring at all the commotion. "Which floor does he live on?" I asked.

"Thirteenth floor," said Gareth, pointing. "You can see all the cables and stuff, how he's wired to the park. Liesl lives just below him. Or she did, anyhow."

"I can't imagine Liesl living here. It's all so . . ."

"Posh," said Gareth, finishing the sentence for me. "Doorman in the lobby, women in fur coats."

There was a stir around the crowd for a moment and someone asked, "Is he coming?" And then the crowd parted and a skinny girl darted out past the doorman and all the people and right past us. Her eyes clicked with mine for a moment, and then she broke into a run. Although her hair was cut short and neat and she was wearing a clean yellow sundress, there was only one person who moved like that. Gareth and I realized it at the same time. "Liesl!" we both yelled, and started to run after her.

But she was long gone.

"Wow, how'd she do that?" Gareth asked. "She doesn't move that fast on the baseball field."

"Must be her haircut. Her hair was weighing her down before."

"And all the dirt's been scrubbed off. She must weigh at least ten pounds less. I wonder what she was doing here?"

I could taste the disappointment in my mouth. I couldn't believe how much I had wanted to see Liesl again.

"We could start passing out petitions," Gareth said.

"Okay," I said.

"We'll start with the store owners right along this street," said Gareth. "They're going to be affected if a mall comes in here."

We went into a ritzy-looking antique store. "Can I help you?" A woman with white hair and a blue dress with a pearl necklace looked up from the newspaper she had been reading. I could see it was the one with the headlines about the park.

"Do you want to sign this petition to keep the park?" Gareth asked.

"This park business is so distressing," she said. Then she read the petition and nodded. "Well, mine will be the first name on the page."

"Thank you," said Gareth, and I felt a surge of hope.

The next person we asked was a big guy at the counter of a leather shop. The store smelled good, the way leather smells, all musty and tingly in your nose, a friendly smell. The guy pounded his fist on the counter when he read the petition. "That's the stuff, guys! We're not going to let this happen!"

Gareth and I looked at each other as we stepped out of the store. "It's going to work," he said excitedly.

The next person we asked was the little old lady in a dry cleaning shop. Her wall was covered with letters from people thanking her for the great job she'd done cleaning their clothes. Even the mayor of Gloria had written her a letter. "I never sign petitions, dear," she said when Gareth asked her. "I just pray and leave it all in the hands of the Lord."

"Well, just this once, could you pray *and* sign the petition?" Gareth asked.

The little old lady laughed, a little chirpy laugh like a happy bird, and signed.

Every single shop owner we asked signed the petition. Then we began stopping random people on the street. Everyone except for one girl signed the petition. She said, "Hey, what's wrong with a mall? It's about time we had some progress around here. Everything'll be in one place, you know, and there'll be a place to park. And it won't matter if it's cold and raining. Personally, I think it's a great idea."

"Personally," said Gareth as she walked away, "I think you're a lazy good-for-nothing example of everything that's wrong with the world. And I'm hungry. Let's go to the park while it still exists and get something to eat. We'll go to Sammy's and get him to sign the petition too."

We went to Sammy's hot dog stand in the park, asking him to sign the petition while we were waiting for the hot dogs. Then we sat on a bench and ate, stuffing the petitions under our legs so that they wouldn't fly away in the breeze. Jerry Rabinowitz came by. He was talking to himself.

"He's trying out one of his poems," said Gareth. He stood up and waved his cap at him. "Hey, Jerry, want to sign a petition to keep the park?"

Jerry came over to us. He was wearing a green bandanna on his head, a green shirt, and green pants. "I've already written a poem about it," he said. "It's called 'The Dog's Lament.' How a dog feels about losing its space, where it walks and runs and plays catch and relieves itself, you know? It goes like this:

> "Green grassy lawns are gone
> My legs no more will stretch
> No more will run
> Although, in heaven, perhaps
> There is for dogs and golfers
> A lawn, eternally green."

He sort of wailed out each word, as if he were a hound dog howling at the moon, and it made the hair on the back of my neck prickle. "We artists don't get into politics, man, but this time you better believe I'm gonna sign." He scribbled his name on the petition and then went on his way, howling out his poem as he went.

Gareth and I sat and finished our hot dogs. I looked around. A hefty-looking young woman pushed an old woman in a wheelchair. A bunch of college-age kids went by with books under their arms. Someone stood on the grass and practiced tai chi. It was hard to believe that in a short time the trees and the statue of Colonel Pettingill and the fountain would be gone and all these people would be inside. Gareth looked at his watch. "You about done? It's almost time for practice."

I nodded, swallowing the last bite of hot dog, and then something yellow caught my eye.

thirteen

I just always thought it would be fun
to have a daughter to buy clothes for.
—*Rebecca Dolittle*

"It's Liesl!" I yelled. This time I wasn't going to let her get away. I raced across the park, my eyes glued to her yellow dress. I caught up to her and grabbed a skinny arm just as she ducked behind a shed.

"Hey, man, let go," Liesl squawked. She tugged and wriggled but I held on.

"You wait a second, Liesl," I yelled. "I want to talk to you for one second."

"I don't want to talk to you." She made a *kkk* sound in her throat.

"If you spit on me, Liesl, I swear I'll spit right back at you." I cleared my throat, making the most disgusting sound I could manage. I narrowed my eyes at her, willing her to back down.

"All right, all right," she said finally. "Let go of me, will you? I'll talk, but I can't stay." As I let go, she looked around nervously. "I ran away and I don't want to get caught."

"You look like . . ." I searched wildly in my mind for what she looked like. "You look like a Christmas tree the day after they took off all the ornaments," I finally said.

"Oh, thanks," she said.

"I mean, all cleaned up and in normal clothes."

"Come on, Willy Wilson, what did you want to talk about, anyway? I don't want to get caught. I don't want to go back to that place."

"Where are you going to go?"

"I don't know. I was thinking about Mitch Bloom. I know he'd let me stay with him. He was thinking about adopting me, remember?"

I was afraid to let her out of my sight. "For right now I think you ought to come home with me," I said. "To Aunt Bridget's. She won't mind. Just try to walk without slouching, so if someone is out looking for you, they won't recognize you."

We poked out from behind the shed and there didn't seem to be anyone around we had to worry about. I looked over to where Gareth had been sitting. He wasn't there anymore. I looked all around for him but didn't see him. He must have gone to practice. Sure enough, in the distance I could see kids on the baseball field, and Toenail's blue hair. I thought I could even hear Gareth shouting insults. He'd be aggravated, all right, ticked at me for running off like that. I'd have to explain everything to him later.

We raced across the park to Aunt Bridget's, up the creaky stairs, and into the apartment. The first thing I saw was a big note pinned to Flora. It said: Dearest Willy, Gone looking for heads. I left you some tuna fish in the fridge. XXOO B.

"You hungry or thirsty or anything?" I asked Liesl.

"Okay," she said in a small voice.

"Okay?"

"I'm hungry and thirsty," she said, still in that small voice. It made me uneasy. She not only didn't look like herself, she didn't sound or act like herself. I made two tuna fish sandwiches and poured two glasses of milk.

When I came back out to the living room, Liesl was sitting on the couch with Sophie in her lap. In the sundress she looked bony and young. "So, what were the Dolittles like?" I asked, handing her a plate with a sandwich on it and glass of milk.

She put the plate on her lap and held the glass with two hands, like a really little kid would have, and drank very quickly. Sophie poked her nose into the sandwich.

"You can push Sophie off, you know," I said.

"I don't want to," said Liesl.

"My mother would have a heart attack if she saw that," I said.

Liesl ate almost all the sandwich, but she left some and put it down on the floor, and Sophie jumped off her lap and finished it up.

"So now can you tell me about the Dolittles?" I asked.

Liesl slipped off the couch and settled herself on the floor, with her back resting against the couch, and held Sophie in her lap. She sighed and made a face. "They were like fungus," she said. "Everywhere I went, they were there. And oh God, her perfume. I thought I was going to die from the stink. I'm telling you, they didn't like the way I talked or walked or ate or even breathed. And they—And they—" She could barely speak. I looked away. I didn't want to see Liesl cry. She stroked Sophie hard and began again. "They knew I liked to draw," she said. "So they gave me these stupid squares of canvas—but they weren't big enough. And they wouldn't get me any chalk. I had to use paint and I don't like paint. You still have my chalk, don't you?" she asked anxiously.

I nodded and went into my room to get the apron and brought it back to her. She grabbed it from me and set it next to her, taking out a few of the chalks, rolling them in her fingers.

"I tried painting the fountain because I was worried because I couldn't see it from their apartment and I missed it. I used to have a great view of it from where I lived before. So I took the paint, even though I didn't like it, and I painted the fountain with all the colors going on at once with these big gushes of color. It got them really mad."

"I don't get it," I said. "Why did it get them mad?"

"I guess they didn't like the paint all over their floor," Liesl said with a sly little smile.

"Oh great, Liesl," I said. "You painted on the floor?"

"I couldn't paint on those stupid little squares," she said. She was cackling now like an old witch. I was so relieved to see she was her old self again, I laughed with her.

"But what about school, Liesl?"

Liesl seemed to shrink inside herself. She clutched Sophie tightly. "I don't want to talk about that." I bit my lip so that I wouldn't say anything more, like, *I told you so,* or *What are you going to do now?* "I don't see how people can stand being in families," she said. "Living all on top of each other. I almost went crazy with the Dolittles."

"I almost go crazy in my own family," I said. It was the first time I had admitted that to anyone. "But all families aren't like mine or the Dolittles'. I bet Gareth has a great family," I said enviously.

"Yeah, but it's a wonder how they can stand *him,*" said Liesl. She gently lifted Sophie off her lap and stood up and stretched. "I need different clothes real bad," she said. "I hate this stinking dress and it's all I have. I tried to get into my apartment this morning but they changed the lock."

"You could always wear a gorilla suit," I said, nodding at Aunt Bridget's sewing table. A few of the finished bodies hung on the back of a chair.

Liesl jumped up and walked over and stroked the black fuzz. "What is all this stuff?"

"Aunt Bridget has to make thirty gorilla suits."

Liesl made a face. "That's a lot of gorillas," she said. She held one of the finished ones up against her body.

"I don't know," I said. "I'm not sure it goes with your hair."

Liesl looked startled for a moment, as if I were being serious, and then she broke out into a little witchy laugh again. "You're funny, Willy Wilson," she said.

"Thank you," I said.

We heard creaking on the stairs, and then Aunt Bridget came in, bursting through the apartment door, and dumped an armful of bags to the floor. "Come and look, Willy," she said. She pulled a gorilla mask out of a bag. "This is rubber, the kind you can get in a drugstore on Halloween. I bought a bunch of them and then I just happened to run into this guy I know who works backstage at the Palace."

Aunt Bridget hadn't even noticed Liesl yet. She dove into another bag and came up with a roll of cloth tape.

"Aunt Bridget—" I started to say. "Aunt Bridget—"

"Larry Lewis is one of the stagehands at the Palace and he said that rubber masks will collapse and tear—this was after I had looked all over town for thirty of them. The way these stores are, you get the idea that people only dress up once a year, on Halloween. I don't understand that—I used to dress up all the time, any time of year. Anyway, Larry told me to get this cloth tape. It's the same stuff you use when you break your leg or something. It's plaster, you know, and you wet it—" She reached into a bag and pulled up a roll of gauzy-looking stuff. "Then I can mold it into gorilla faces and when it dries, I can paint it. Pretty nifty, don't you think?"

"Aunt Bridget." I took Aunt Bridget's arm and pulled her away from the bags and positioned her right in front of Liesl.

"Oh my goodness!" Aunt Bridget exclaimed. "Liesl! I'm so sorry, I was so full of my masks I didn't see you, and even if I had seen you, I'm not sure I would have recognized you right away. You look so . . ."

Liesl crossed her skinny arms. "Your nephew says I look like a Christmas tree after all the ornaments have been taken off."

Aunt Bridget put back her head and roared. "He's a funny one, that nephew. I, however, think you look very nice. That short hair suits you. And your dress—it's very well made, simple but expensive," she said with a professional tone. "How is your new family working out?"

Liesl hung on to the back of the chair and stared at Aunt Bridget with her large eyes.

"It didn't work out," I said, speaking for her. "She, um, ran away."

Aunt Bridget put down the roll of tape and put her hands on her hips and really looked at Liesl. "Well," she finally said.

Liesl didn't say a word, but she swallowed and blinked.

"I could use your artistic ability with the making of these masks," Aunt Bridget said. "That'll keep you busy—just until we can figure out the next step. We'll have to get in touch with Otto Pettingill, of course. What on earth is the matter with that man, casting you off into the world, and then this idiotic business of selling the park?"

"Selling the park?"

My stomach dropped as I saw Liesl turn very pale, and the blue vein began to throb. She balled her hands into angry fists. "That stinking, freaking man!" she hissed. "He can't do that. He can't sell the park!" She started hitting the air, and then she kicked the chair, sending gorilla costumes flying. Scared, I moved away, but Aunt Bridget rushed over and threw her arms around her.

"Hush," said Aunt Bridget as Liesl struggled for a moment. "It's all right, Liesl. We'll figure out something. We will, we really will. Red, red, red," she said slowly and softly, "green, green, green, yellow, yellow, yellow, blue."

"What?" said Liesl. She pushed away from Aunt Bridget, looking at her as if she were crazy.

Aunt Bridget took her by the hand and led her to the window. It was just dusk, dark enough for the fountain lights to be on. The plumes of color gushed up. Red, red, red, green, green, green, yellow, yellow, yellow, blue.

"We'll figure out something," said Aunt Bridget again. "First of all, we need to contact Mr. Pettingill. In the meantime, Liesl, I want you to stay here. And you know you really can be a great help with the gorillas. Come on, let's get started."

We set up a gorilla factory. I cut, Aunt Bridget

sewed, and Liesl worked on the masks. We made three in all. It was a very hairy experience.

Afterward, when Liesl was calmer, Aunt Bridget looked up the Dolittles' number in the phone book. "I have to let them know you're safe," Aunt Bridget said when Liesl squealed in protest. "Can you believe it? There are five Dolittles in the city of Gloria. You don't have any idea of what their first names are, do you?"

"Yes," said Liesl.

"Well, do you want to tell me?"

"No," said Liesl. Aunt Bridget waggled her eyebrows at her and Liesl sighed. "Rory and Rebecca. They were matching, just like the clothes they wore."

"Rory and Rebecca," Aunt Bridget muttered, running a finger down the page. "Here they are." Liesl rocked slightly as Aunt Bridget tried the number. "No go," she said. "It's busy." Liesl grinned like a maniac.

Next Aunt Bridget tried calling Mr. Pettingill. The phone was disconnected. Then she tried Mr. Brookings. "I don't want to," she said, "but it's the responsible thing to do." But only his office number was listed and no one was answering there.

"You could leave a message," I said, not enthusiastically.

"I could," said Aunt Bridget, also not enthusiastically. "I don't like talking to answering machines. I have a sort of phobia about it."

"If you reach any of these people, don't you have to say where I am?" Liesl asked. "And then won't they come and get me?"

"Not if I tell them they have to wait," said Aunt Bridget. She tried the Dolittles again. "Still busy. I'll try them later. It's getting late and we've worked hard. It's time to eat."

We ate (Chinese food again), and after that Liesl went through the costume boxes in my room and tried on half the stuff and laughed like a lunatic. Then she sat on my bed, Sophie curled up next to her.

"What's that?" she asked, nodding at my violin case.

"My violin," I said.

"Why don't you play it?"

I made a face. "I'm not very good," I said.

"You're chicken," she said. "You're chicken about everything."

I sighed. "Okay, I'll prove how bad I am." I opened the case and took out the violin and bow. "Here goes nothing," I said, sticking it under my chin and swiping the bow across the strings. I winced. "Kind of out of tune." I sat on the bed and began tuning it. I was never very good at that, either, never sure I really could tune it on my own. Liesl was right. I was a chicken about so many things—I mean, how could I be afraid of even tuning a violin? I plucked the strings. Okay, that sounded okay. I'd just pretend it was tuned, even if I wasn't sure.

Standing up, I played the best thing I could play. It was an easy version of Pachelbel's Canon. The first few notes were pretty shaky, but as I was playing, this idea jumped into my mind: that each swipe of the bow across the strings was like creating a piece of gold thread, and pretty soon all the pieces of gold thread made a golden ball, and the golden ball was what made the whole song, and then by playing the song, I was sending out the ball for other people to catch. I finished the piece and before Liesl could even know I had finished it, I started over again. It was better the second time through. I think it was the first time I had ever played a whole song through by myself without my mother. It sounded much better without her.

Aunt Bridget came and leaned in the doorway. She had tears in her eyes. "That was beautiful, Willy."

"You're not too bad," Liesl said.

I felt my face turn hot and even my hands were sweaty with a kind of happiness. I wanted to play the piece again, to play it three hundred more times. It made me think of Otto Pettingill—I could see why he liked to stand in his apartment and send his music out into the park.

"How long have you been playing?" Aunt Bridget asked.

"Not very long," I said.

"Well, you should keep at it," she said. "You have a very nice tone."

My heart pumped extra hard. I thought: *I might be good at this*.

And on top of that thought was another secret: *I might even like this*.

"The Dolittles aren't answering and they don't have an answering machine," said Aunt Bridget. "It's late and I'm not calling them again. Liesl, you'll be comfy on the couch in the living room. At least for tonight you're not going anywhere."

"Goody," said Liesl.

"We can get in touch with Mr. Brookings in the morning."

I didn't tell Aunt Bridget, but I had already decided Liesl and I should go there in person, right to his office. We were going to go there and ask him where Otto Pettingill was, so we could tell him three things: he had to keep the park, he had to start playing music again, and he had to let Mitch Bloom adopt Liesl.

I groaned a little inwardly. Put like that, it sounded ridiculous. How could two kids convince Otto Pettingill to do all that? I stayed awake for a long time, whispering out loud the stirring speeches I was going to make to Mr. Pettingill.

fourteen

The most important thing
is to have teeth that can chew.

—Old Violet

Nothing like speech-making to keep you up at night. I didn't wake up the next morning until ten. Aunt Bridget sent Liesl to wake me up. She, I noticed, had little black hairs all over her face from sleeping on the couch.

"We're going to find Mr. Roland Brookings," I announced at the breakfast table. I had the telephone book in front of me. I found his office address. It was in the West Park. "We're going to tell him you didn't like the Dolittles and we're going to find Mr. Pettingill and talk to him in person."

"What if he decides to lock me up and throw me into a dark cellar with rats and starve me to death?" Liesl asked. Hunched over a cereal bowl, she was eating the last box of cereal. First she slurped the milk into her mouth and then she began chewing with her mouth open.

"There's a good chance he will," I said, watching her with disgust. For the first time in my life, I was grateful that my mother was so naggy about manners.

"I'd like to come with you," said Aunt Bridget. "Although I'm afraid I'm not the sort of grown-up an important person like Roland Brookings pays much attention to." She frowned for a moment and then said, "What about Mitch Bloom?"

Liesl clapped her hands. "Mitch Bloom would be perfect. I've seen him act like a real grown-up lots of times."

Aunt Bridget waggled her eyebrows at Liesl. "You think I don't know how," she said with a smile. "I can read you like a book, Liesl; no point in trying to hide your thoughts from me. Well, I wish we could finish a few gorillas before you go, but you better skedaddle."

"Your aunt is great," said Liesl as we walked through the park on our way to find Mitch. "And I liked making those gorilla heads."

"They turned out pretty good," I said.

"Of course," she said. She skipped as she said it, very conceited.

"You're supposed to say *thanks*," I said. "*Thank you very much*. That's what civilized people say when you say something nice to them."

"You're getting bossy, just like Gareth," she said.

"Oh my God, Gareth!" I said with a groan. "I ran out on yesterday's practice and I was going to call him last night and I forgot."

"He'll be burned—ripped—loco—cuckoo—nutso," Liesl said happily. "And the game against the Sharks is coming up."

"Yeah, but the park might be *gone* in two days," I said, the reality of the situation hitting me like a jolt. I felt another jolt as we neared Mitch Bloom's flower stand and I saw that it was closed up. GONE TO COLLECT MORE PETITIONS, a sign said. WE WILL SAVE THE PARK.

I stared at the sign with dismay. "Now what?" I said.

"Hey, Willy Wilson, don't be a wimp. We'll go there by ourselves. What's the big deal?"

"Okay," I said. I didn't feel as if we had any choice.

"Why do you think he was trying to get rid of me?" Liesl asked as we walked away.

"Who was trying to get rid of you?"

"Mr. Creep Pettingill."

"He's not a creep," I said. "He knew you weren't happy. He was trying to *make* you happy. He knew you wanted to go to school."

Liesl kicked a piece of gravel and didn't say anything.

"We could ask Old Violet to come with us," I said as we neared her bench.

"Yeah." Liesl giggled. "She could look at Roland Brookings and say, 'What a big jerk you are, *ha!*'"

Just as she said this, Old Violet reached a bony hand out and grabbed Liesl by the arm. Her voice was old and creaky, as if it wasn't used very much. "What a big girl you are, *ha!*" she screeched. "You see my teeth? Perfect, ain't they?" She smiled a big smile. They were pretty good teeth, all white and straight. Somehow surprising in that wrinkly old face. "You ain't got teeth like that, Liesl Summer, on account of not brushing them. On account of that Mr. Pettingill leaving you all alone in an apartment with only Belle Vera to take care of you. And everyone knows Belle Vera, what she's like."

Liesl stamped a foot. "Don't you be dissing Belle Vera to me," she fumed. "You don't know anything about her and that's a fact."

"I know she got fired from her job before she got you, that's what I know. She was a schoolteacher, and they fired her."

"They didn't fire her, they retired her," said Liesl.

"Fired, retired, not much difference that I can see."

"You be quiet, Old Violet."

"Don't you be calling me old, you hear me?" Old Violet screeched.

"Come on, Liesl, let's go." I pulled her by the arm. Old Violet was skinny and she was old, but she looked mighty wiry and she was getting all worked up. I could imagine her giving Liesl a good belt in the mouth.

"Don't you be calling me old!" Old Violet screeched again as we ran away.

"Good grief, if this place is turned into a mall, what will happen to her?"

"I don't care what happens to her," Liesl said hotly. "I hope she falls down dead and rots and dies. I hope her teeth fall out and her gums turn black. Do you want to know something?"

"I guess," I said, not very enthusiastically.

"The only reason Old Violet is alive at all is because of Belle Vera. She pays for her apartment and her food and everything."

That was a shocker. I stopped dead still and stared at Liesl. "Really? But how?"

Liesl put her hands on her hips. "You think Belle Vera is poor, don't you? That she was living off what Otto Pettingill paid her to take care of me?"

I nodded. "I guess I thought something like that."

"When she lived in France she had a ton of money. Then the Nazis came, but her family got out in time and socked all their money into a Swiss bank. Belle Vera is loaded."

I shook my head. "How do you know all this?"

"I hear things," Liesl said with a big grin.

"But why does Old Violet hate her so much, then?"

"Old Violet doesn't *know*. And Old Violet is an old witch. She doesn't like anyone, but she especially doesn't like Belle Vera because Belle Vera is nice to her."

"Like you, huh?" The words shot out before I could stop them. I held my breath, waiting for one of Liesl's tantrums, but she was standing very still and her eyes seemed very watery.

"I didn't appreciate Belle Vera until I got adopted," she said in a small voice. "And I'm not like Old Violet—I'm not."

"I didn't say you were," I said.

"Yes you did," she said.

"Come on, Liesl," I said, pulling her by the arm. "We're never going to get anywhere just standing here."

We continued on through the park, keeping our eyes open for the Dolittles. Meanwhile, I was getting more and more nervous. I kept thinking of new things. "The Dolittles have probably already told Mr. Brookings that you ran away," I said as we neared the Pettingill Building.

"Yeah," said Liesl. "So what's your point?"

I sighed. So she was back to being a tough kid. Okay. That was my punishment for getting to see her be soft and nice for half a minute. "My point is, maybe he's going to be mad about it. Maybe he's not going to be so nice. Maybe you should lie low and maybe I should go by myself to try to find out where Mr. Pettingill is, and then we should go find him and tell him you want to live with Mitch."

"Yeah, but that means I don't get to tell Roland Brookings what I think of him and his Dolittles."

I sighed again. There wasn't much point in trying to reason with Liesl, but as we approached the west side, I wished Mitch, or even Aunt Bridget, was with us.

In the lobby of the Pettingill Building, we found a listing of the offices. Roland Brookings' office was on the sixth floor. We punched the button for the elevator and then stood there waiting and waiting.

Standing around waiting was making me way too jumpy.

"Let's walk up," I said. We found the right door and our footsteps echoed in the hollow stairwell as we went up. We pushed through a heavy door marked SIX and then moved along a hallway of offices. Some of the doors were shut, but some were partially open, and we could see people working at their desks. And then finally we found a glass partition marked ROLAND N. BROOKINGS JR. Looking through it, we could see a receptionist sitting at a desk.

"May I help you?" she asked softly as we opened the glass door and walked in. The name on her desk was Ms. Farren.

"W-we want to see M-Mr. Brookings," I stammered. The whole place reminded me of my father's office, and it made me feel young and like I needed a haircut or my shirt had stains all over it.

"Do you have an appointment?" she asked even more softly. "Mr. Brookings doesn't see anyone without an appointment. He's a busy man." Her eyes flicked to the appointment book in front of her, and my eyes flicked there too. I saw only one name marked down for that day: Frank Featherstone. Frank Featherstone was the guy who wanted to buy the park and turn it into a mall.

fifteen

When I get to feeling down,
I look at the flower on my ankle.
It cheers me up—I don't know why,
but, like, anyhow, who cares why?

—Karen Farren

"Who did you say you were?" Ms. Farren asked as we just stood in front of her, not saying anything.

I saw Liesl take a breath, ready to blurt out her name. I quickly jumped in. "Excuse us a minute," I said. I took Liesl by the arm and pulled her out of the waiting area and back into the main hallway where Ms. Farren wouldn't be able to see us. The base of my neck felt prickly. The office was so formal, with its blue couch and blue chairs and gleaming glass coffee table. It even smelled like an Important Place.

It made me think of Roland Brookings and his brief-case. Now more than ever I was sure he wasn't going to be pleased that Liesl had painted on the Dolittles' floor and then run away.

"Don't tell her who you are," I whispered urgently. "Not yet. Let's see if we can find out how Roland Brookings is feeling about you first."

"I do have a lot of work to do, so if you could—" Ms. Farren's washed-out voice faded completely as we came back in.

I decided that someone who sounded like that couldn't really be mean. If I could only figure out a way to get her to help us.

"We're actually waiting for Mr. Featherstone," I blurted out. I tried to catch Liesl's eye. "He's our dad." I could feel my face turning red and my heart bumped uncomfortably.

"Your dad?" Ms. Farren looked at me in surprise.

"He said to meet us here at twelve-thirty," I said, trying to read the appointment book upside down.

"But he won't be here until one," said Ms. Farren. She pointed a chewed nail at the appointment book. A person who bit her nails couldn't be too sure of herself, I, Detective Wilson, thought. The way she was sitting, rolled back from her desk and a bit to one side, I could see she had a tattoo right above her left ankle. It was a flower. A person who had a flower tattoo wouldn't stick completely to the rules, I, Detective Wilson, decided.

I rocked on my heels to get the shakes out of my legs. "He said twelve-thirty, I know he did," I said. I nudged Liesl. "Didn't he?"

"Yup, twelve-thirty," she said. I was so glad the Dolittles had cleaned her up so she looked halfway normal. And lying was no big deal for Liesl, that was for sure. She didn't look nervous at all.

"And he told us to come straight here and not move or we'd be in big trouble. *Big* trouble," I repeated.

"Goodness," lisped Ms. Farren. "I would hate to see such nice-looking kids as the two of you getting into trouble. Now, that Liesl Summer is a different case."

Liesl stiffened and I stepped in front of her, trying to hide her. I turned my hand into a fist behind my back and shook it at Liesl.

"Oh, that kid," I said. "What a mess!"

"The poor little thing," said Ms. Farren. "And Mr. Brookings is fit to be tied. I wouldn't want to be around when he finally gets his hands on her."

"What do you mean?" I asked.

"Mr. Brookings placed her with a very nice family and she ran away from them."

"Huh!" I said. "That's a heck of a way to show her gratitude." I could feel Liesl breathing hard behind me.

"Well, maybe the family wasn't as nice as all that, who knows, but I wouldn't want Mr. Brookings to hear me say that." She cringed slightly, looking over her shoulder. "Actually, I feel sorry for the girl. I mean, she can't help being a mess, can she? But anyhow, if you're going to wait for your father, you'd better sit and wait over there." She pointed to the blue couch across from her desk. "But you've got to be quiet. Mr. Brookings doesn't like kids hanging about the place. He has very important work to do." She glanced nervously over her shoulder at a closed door just behind her. *Aha! Brookings' office,* I thought. Then she picked up a folder and opened it and began staring at it as if it was very important and interesting.

Liesl and I sat down on the blue couch. I waggled my eyebrows at her in an Aunt Bridget sort of way.

"What if he comes in and sees me?" Liesl hissed. "I can't stay here."

"We can't leave without finding out where Mr. Pettingill is," I hissed back.

My mind was spinning. What *would* Mr. Brookings do when he saw Liesl? Maybe he wouldn't recognize her. Wouldn't it be better if I went in and spoke to him by myself? Without thinking, I picked up a magazine from the coffee table in front of us. It was a business magazine, full of graphs. My dad was always reading magazines like that.

"Ms. Farren," I said, "you don't know where Mr. Pettingill is, do you?"

"Oh no." She laughed. "Only Mr. Brookings knows that. A real mystery man, he is." She poked her nose out from behind her folder. "I have a little girl just about your age," she said, smiling at Liesl.

Aha! She was deciding to be friendly. I, Detective Wilson, had been right about her.

"You're a bit shy, though, aren't you, sweetheart?" Ms. Farren asked. "My little girl, Melissa, was real shy, too, but she's growing out of it. What's your name, honey?"

"Lie—"

"Rooty," I said, my eye catching something in the magazine about the roots of economic depression. "Short for Ruth," I added when Liesl kicked me. I put down the magazine. I had figured out what to do. All I needed now was courage.

"Since we have to stay here for a while, do you think Rooty could have something to draw with?" I asked, getting up and walking over to Ms. Farren's desk.

"Of course." Ms. Farren pulled a few pieces of paper from a printer tray. Then she opened a drawer in her desk and poked through it. "And here are some colored pencils," she said. "I keep them for Melissa when she has to wait here. You'd think he could be a little more understanding." Ms. Farren made a face and nodded in the direction of the closed door. "I'm a single mother, but do you think *he* cares?" Her faded voice grew a shade louder.

"I know how it is. My mom's a single mom, too," I said. The minute I said it, I knew it was the wrong thing. What in the world had made me say that?

Ms. Farren looked puzzled. "But—"

"I mean, she was," I said, panic sending my heart bumping again. What a jerk I was. In trying to be sympathetic, I had blown it. What a mistake. "I mean, she was until she married Frank Featherstone. Then he adopted us."

"Oh, I see," said Ms. Farren. "Well, your mother's a lucky woman, that's all I can say."

I went back to Liesl with the pencils and paper. "Rooty?" Liesl snarled under her breath. "Dodo," she said in a high, whiny voice, "can I have a drink of water?"

"Dodo?" Ms. Farren smiled. "Is that your name?"

"Dudley," I said. I glared at Liesl. "She could never pronounce it."

"Well, Dudley," said Ms. Farren, "there's a water cooler down the hall, but go quietly or Mr. B. will kill me. He's been preparing for this meeting with your father all week."

"I sure hope my dad gets the park," I said, feeling reckless now that I had gotten away with my mistake.

Ms. Farren sighed. "Some people in the world always get what they want. I expect your father is one of them."

I glanced at the clock behind Ms. Farren's head. It was almost one. It was time to get this show on the road. I went down the hallway to the water cooler, making up my mind to put my plan into action when I came back.

Handing Liesl a cup of water, I whispered, "Draw the best portrait you can of her." Then I sat on the couch and waited, the palms of my hands turning sweatier and sweatier. Minutes passed. *"Hurry up,"* I muttered through my teeth. Actually, it was amazing how in a couple of quick strokes, Liesl had gotten the shape of Ms. Farren's long, thin face, her short nose, and her scraggily long hair, and also her sort of helpless, saggy look. I knelt beside her. "Perfect," I whispered. "I'm getting her over here and then we can convince her that if she has a photo you can do a perfect portrait of Melissa. I'm going into Mr. Brookings' office now."

Liesl didn't look up. Her long fingers just kept moving. "Ms. Farren," I said. "You should take a break from your work and come and see Rooty's picture of you. It's really good. I'm just going to get more water, okay?"

"I could use a break," Ms. Farren said. She pushed back from her chair and came over to the blue couch. "Now let's see your nice picture, sweetheart."

I walked quickly past Ms. Farren. I darted behind her desk. As my hand turned the doorknob to Roland Brookings Jr.'s door, I heard Ms. Farren squeal, "Why, goodness gracious! Will you look at that! Did you draw this picture all by yourself?"

"Yes? What is it, Ms. Farren?" Mr. Brookings' voice came from the floor. He was crouched over the bottom drawer of a filing cabinet. I shut the door and then turned. All I could see was Mr. Brookings' back. He wasn't wearing the white suit jacket—just a white shirt. "Give me a minute, Ms. Farren," he ordered.

I sat down in a big leather armchair in front of his large desk. I was glad to have a minute to calm down. I tried to focus on what was around me. The walls were covered with paintings, and after a bit I realized they were scenes of the park: there was the fountain, the statue of Colonel Pettingill on his horse, and even one of the baseball field with kids playing baseball on it. I thought of Gareth again and sighed.

More than a few minutes went by. Mr. Brookings remained kneeling on the floor, grumbling to himself as he fumbled through the drawer. "Just hang on, Ms. Farren," he said aloud.

When he finally stood up and turned around and saw me, he gasped, and then his face turned bright red, almost as red as his hair. He leaned threateningly toward me. "I told your mother not to let kids in here," he said nastily. "You go and tell her I want to see her immediately."

He doesn't recognize me, I thought. There were advantages to being invisible to older people. To me, though, those cold blue glaring eyes were only too familiar.

"Don't just stand there," Mr. Brookings snapped.

I began rocking on my heels. Rocking really did help keep my legs from shaking too badly. "Excuse me," I started to say. "I just—"

"I suppose your mother thinks if I see you it'll soften my heart so I'll help her with her messy divorce." He picked up a silver letter opener from his desk and jabbed the air with it. "Well, you can tell her I don't want anything to do with it, do you hear?" He stepped out from behind his desk and towered over me, that letter opener scarily close to my face. I could see orange hair on his freckly knuckles. *"Now get out!"*

My legs felt like water. They weren't even strong enough to carry me out of the room. "But do you know where Mr. Pettingill is?" I asked weakly.

"Get out of here before I call the police!" Mr. Brookings shouted.

"Roland!" A man in a navy blue blazer strode into the room. I stared at him and he stared at me. In those few seconds, I had this impression of gold. I think the glasses he was wearing were gold-rimmed. And there were all these gold buttons on his blazer, up and down the front and on his cuffs. Then I melted out the door, but before it closed, something made me leap back into the room and duck down behind one of the armchairs.

"Frank," Mr. Brookings was saying, his tone of voice totally changed. "How nice to see you."

sixteen

*I've always wondered what it would be like
to hit a golf ball made of gold
with a golf club made of gold.*
—*Frank Featherstone*

"Hope you don't mind if I'm a bit early," said the man. I knew he had to be Frank Featherstone. "Your secretary wasn't around, so I just trotted myself in here."

"She's going to find herself *completely* not around if she keeps this up," Mr. Brookings muttered. "In any case, Frank, of course I'm delighted to see you. Do sit down." He sounded so calm and agreeable, I could hardly believe he was the same guy who had been shouting his head off at me a moment ago.

I hugged myself into as small a ball as possible as the khaki pant legs of Frank Featherstone settled themselves a few inches from me. The only thing between me and them was the back of the chair. Where had Ms. Farren been when Frank Featherstone had come in? I wondered. What a stroke of luck she hadn't been there. Ms. Farren would have said, "Here's your darling little girl," and Frank Featherstone would have said, "What? She's not my darling little girl." I shuddered. I didn't even want to think about what would have happened next.

"So here we are," Frank Featherstone said.

"I'm going to make sure that door is shut," said Mr. Brookings. I bit my lip. He passed right by me. He could have tripped over me. He opened and then shut the door firmly, and then walked right by me again. "That was one of my secretary's brats—that boy you saw when you arrived. He just walked right in here, didn't even knock. Walked right in, can you believe that?"

"I saw another kid out there when I came in," said Mr. Featherstone.

"Ms. Farren's more trouble than she's worth," Mr. Brookings grumbled. "I'm going to sack her as soon as we're finished with this business."

I stared at Mr. Featherstone's shoes. They were a funny color. Yellowish greenish brownish with dots and squiggles. Maybe they were snakeskin, or alligator. Whatever they were, they looked expensive. What if I squirmed my hand under the chair and grabbed one of the shoelaces? Just yanked on one? Wouldn't Frank Featherstone be surprised? He crossed his legs. His shoes and his shoelaces were out of reach, but now his arm hung down. I could see more gold. Two rings on one hand: a wedding band and a big klunker on his pinkie. There was a gold bracelet around his wrist, the letters *F. F.* bumped into it in gold. The buttons on the cuffs had golfers on them, golf clubs raised in the middle of the most perfect swing ever.

"So, no problems so far, eh, Rollie?" Mr. Featherstone asked.

"Well, unfortunately, Frank, we may have one."

"And what might that be?" Mr. Featherstone asked.

"Well, as you know, Frank," said Mr. Brookings, and I could hear him sigh before he went on, "up until now, O. P. has played right into our hands. O. P. trusted my father with all the business closest to his heart. It was, you know, my father who helped create the park—they spent days and days designing the fountain so that the water would gush up in the same rhythm as a Mozart sonata. They thought people would like that. They thought people would like grass and trees and music. But I think they were wrong, Frank. I think what people want is *things*."

"Huh!" grunted Mr. Featherstone.

"Well, O. P. has finally come to the same conclusion himself," said Mr. B. "'They don't need to have their tastes dictated by me,' he said. 'What people really want is to be free to hear whatever they want to hear.'"

"I know all that," said Mr. Featherstone, sounding a bit irritated and impatient.

"He wanted to go into retirement, disappear, become anonymous. He thought he'd failed with the park, failed with the child. He asked me, if no one raised a fuss, to sell the park, and he asked me to find a home for Liesl."

"Yes, right," said Mr. Featherstone. "He said if there was no protest as of midnight tonight, then the park was to be sold to the highest bidder, and you've taken care of that. And you found a home for the child. So that's jolly ducks then, all our jolly ducks are in a row." Mr. Featherstone brought his feet together with a sort of slap, as if he were clapping them instead of his hands. "I don't see what the problem could be."

"It's the child," said Mr. Brookings. "You may recall that O. P. came to my office, not long after my father passed on, and told me he thought he had made a colossal mistake in raising the girl the way he had. He said, 'She's full of life and full of energy—what I always wanted for her. And how she can draw! But she is a wild child, thoroughly uncivilized.' I wanted to laugh in his face. What had he expected? 'And what a bad temper she has,' he complained. But the worst of it for him was that she never learned to read. He thought she would have been able to teach herself."

Liesl couldn't read! I was shocked. I hadn't thought about it. It had never occurred to me that someone Liesl's age wouldn't be able to read. No wonder she sat so still when Mitch Bloom read to her.

"So," Mr. Brookings went on, "the old man realizes the kid is unhappy because she has never been allowed to go to school. So now, he comes to me. 'Find her a family,' he says. 'Find her a school.' Well, I admit I am not as imaginative as my father, but there is no reason why I couldn't find a decent situation for her. The Dolittles were perfectly good people. The East Park Day School is a very good school—where I would have liked to have gone, by the way. Of course, her not being able to read posed a bit of a problem at first, but I'm a trustee of the school, and I was able to make arrangements."

Mr. F. didn't say anything. His feet tapped impatiently, though.

"My father could have afforded to send me anywhere, but no, the roughest school in the city was where I went." I could hear the bitterness in Mr. Brookings' voice. It sounded funny, a grown man complaining about his father. "It didn't matter that I was beaten up every day," he went on. It almost sounded as if he was going to cry. "Roland Brookings' son was supposed to be like everyone else and not be treated special just because his father happened to have money. And our house, too, had to be shabby."

Mr. Featherstone's shoes began to move around a little more, crossing and uncrossing, tapping and swaying.

I tried to shift my position slightly. I was getting cramped, crouched behind the chair, but I sure was getting an earful.

"Are you trying to tell me Liesl didn't like the family?" Mr. Featherstone finally asked. "She'll come around, or at any rate, she'll have to do what they say."

"No, that's the point. She ran away, and I can't find the brat. And if O. P. should hear of this, he'll come out of retirement or hiding or whatever it is he thinks he's doing. He'll catch on to what we're up to—he's not a stupid man."

"Yes, I see," said Mr. Featherstone. "He might discover that we encouraged Mitch Bloom to circulate petitions with the idea that we'd dump 'em in the dumpster."

Holy cow! I thought. Poor Mitch. And poor all the people of the park who had signed those petitions. I was so mad I wanted to spit.

"He might discover that you and I together made a bid so high no one could possibly top it. So—we have to find the girl and help her keep her mouth shut." I felt a chill run down the back of my neck.

"Unfortunately, the Dolittles cleaned her up," said Mr. Brookings. "They cut her hair and so forth, so she's not as recognizable as she used to be. But fortunately they did get her to sit still long enough so they could take her picture. Before this day is over, every cop in town will have a copy of that picture."

Featherstone stood up and began pacing. "How soon can we get those pictures out to the cops?"

"They're working on it now."

I felt cold and clammy with fear. Somehow I had to get myself out of there, and then get Liesl out of there. I started inching my way toward the door.

"At least she's going to have a hard time finding the old man," said Mr. Brookings. "That buys us time."

"Where is he hiding out these days?"

Mr. B. snorted his nasty snort. "At the Heliotrope Café," he said. "Can you believe it? He's hanging out, living above the bar, pretending to be a starving artist or something. He said he wanted to play for a live audience. He figures he's been out of circulation for so long no one'll recognize him, especially not in that part of town."

"What are we going to do with her when we do find her?"

"She's going to stay with *me,*" said Mr. B. I could practically hear his teeth gnashing. "Until the sale absolutely comes through. And then I'll convince the old man to put her in an orphanage or a foster home. And in the meantime, maybe I can teach her some manners."

I held my breath and started sliding my body backwards, preparing to escape. And then there was a soft knocking on the door. A flustered Ms. Farren burst in.

"Ms. Farren!" Mr. Brookings roared. "How dare you?"

"Willy Wilson, where are you?" Liesl pushed past Ms. Farren and then stopped dead in her tracks and squealed when she saw me on the floor. "Oh, there you are. What are you doing?"

"What in the name of all that's—Oh my God, Frank, there she is!"

"Run!" I shouted, leaping up from the floor. I shoved Liesl out of the room and slammed the door. "Run, go, shut up!" I shouted at her and then pushed her through the reception room and down the hallway to the stairs. Was I ever glad we hadn't come up in the elevator so I knew just where those stairs were. Yanking open the heavy fire door, I flung Liesl ahead of me.

"Hey, you, come back here!" Mr. Brookings was pounding after us.

Voices, footsteps, the hammering of my heart, all seemed to echo in the stairwell. My legs were like jelly. I had this enormous urge to lie down and go to sleep. At some point, I don't know when or where, I realized I wasn't pushing Liesl anymore. She was pulling *me*.

Outside, I collapsed against the side of the building. I was dizzy and panicky. Liesl pulled on my arm. "Come on!" she said. "We can run faster than those fat toads any old day."

Her grin lit a spark inside me. I was able to move again. Halfway across the park, she turned to look at me. "Hey, Willy Wilson," she said with that big grin of hers again, "this is cool."

seventeen

Kids only need to learn two things:
how to swim and how to ride a bike.

—*Otto Pettingill*

Inside the apartment at last, I collapsed onto the couch, Liesl onto the floor. My legs hurt, my chest ached, my tongue tasted of car exhaust. "I don't see how people in chase scenes keep going," I gasped.

"How come we're being chased, anyhow?" Liesl asked, her face blazing with excitement.

"They've got all the cops in town out looking for you. At least they won't think to look for us here." I glanced up at Flora and there was an Aunt Bridget note for me. "Gone looking for hands. Hope your mission was successful. XXOO B."

"So what were you doing in that office all that time? And why were you on the floor when I came in?" Liesl asked. Sophie walked by and rubbed against her legs, and Liesl reached over and scooped her up into her lap. "I never had pets," she said. "I don't know why. I guess I didn't want to take care of them. The next place I live I'm going to have cats. Lots of them."

Neither of us said anything for a moment. It was a big question mark, the next place she was going to live. I guess neither of us really knew how to think about it.

"I had to keep talking to that dumb Ms. Farren," she said finally. "She treated me like I was six years old and we kept having to talk about Melissa. Melissa sounds like the most boring excuse for a child that ever existed. And then what was the deal about running out of there?"

I wanted to tell Liesl everything I had overheard in the conversation between Brookings and Featherstone, but there had been a lot, and I had to think about where to begin. I sat still for moment. I could hear all the city sounds coming in the window, but no music.

"Otto Pettingill is hiding out at the Heliotrope Café, playing music there."

"Oh," said Liesl.

"We have to go and find him, right away. Now." I leaped up but my legs buckled and I fell back onto the couch.

"Whoa," said Liesl. "Take it easy there. What's the hurry?"

"Otto Pettingill thought nobody cared about the park anymore, and he decided he'd put it up for sale and give people a chance to protest. So Mitch did, you know, with the petitions and stuff. But Roland Brookings, his lawyer—"

"Duh, I know he's his lawyer," Liesl interrupted.

"I know you know that. I'm just trying to tell you about it so it makes sense, so let me talk." I deliberately stood up and walked into the kitchen and got myself a glass of water. She could wait to hear the rest.

"Come on, Willy Wilson, spit it out," she whined.

I smiled. Taking my time, I poured her some water, too, and came back into the living room. "Roland Brookings secretly wants the park for himself, so he's gone in with Frank Featherstone. Together they've made the offer so big no one can outbid them, but Mr. Pettingill doesn't know Mr. Brookings is doing this."

"Oh, the *cochon*!" Liesl fumed.

"The *what*?"

"It's French for 'pig.' Belle Vera says you aren't supposed to call people that, but it's what she calls Old Violet. I've heard her mutter it under her breath."

"But meanwhile he's afraid Mr. Pettingill's going to find out you didn't like the family he placed you with, and that's going to make him come out of hiding, and then he's going to find out about the deal with Frank Featherstone. So he, Mr. Brookings, doesn't want you running around. He's going to make sure every cop in Gloria has a picture of you— the cleaned-up version of Liesl Summer. He wants to find you and stick you into a foster home far away so you won't cause him any trouble."

"Those Dolittles gave my picture to him?" Liesl's face turned blotchy, and she got up off the floor and began to walk around the living room in circles. "He's going to send me to a foster home?"

"We have to get to the Heliotrope Café. Have you ever heard of it, Liesl?"

She nodded. "I know where everything is. It's in the South Park."

"Well, let's go, then."

"Willy Wilson, you are a moron!" she said, glaring at me with her hands on her hips. "How can I leave this apartment when every cop in Gloria has a picture of me?"

I slapped my forehead. "Oh yeah, I *am* a moron." We both stared at each other for a moment. "We could call Gareth and ask him to go to the café for us."

"I guess," said Liesl, not enthusiastically. "If he can tear himself away from his baseball."

I looked up Gareth's number in the phone book. Luckily there was only one Pugh in the whole city of Gloria. His sister answered the phone. No, Gareth wasn't home.

"No go," I said as I hung up the phone. "He's probably moved away. Probably moved to Yankee Stadium." I stared at Aunt Bridget's note. "Maybe when my aunt gets back she can go for us. If she feels like she can get away from the gorillas."

My eyes rested on the gorilla suits and then the

masks Liesl had made. I looked over at Liesl. She was staring in that direction, too.

"Hey!" Liesl and I spoke at the exact same moment.

We both made a move toward the masks. I slipped one on and started leaping around the living room, grunting and banging my chest with my fists. Then I stepped into one of the pajama gorilla suits. "This is how we're going to get to the Heliotrope Café," I said. "No one'll know it's us."

Liesl was scrambling into another suit. I took one look at her and started to laugh. "What is the matter with you?" she asked. She put her hands on her hips in that Liesl way of hers, but she had the mask on and she looked so ridiculous.

"It's just—It's just—" I gasped through the laughter. "It's just that you look like *you* even when you are a gorilla."

"Oh thanks a lot," she said, stamping her foot, and that set me off again. She pulled the mask off her face. "Will you stop that?"

One look at her blotchy face and I knew she was revving up for a tantrum.

"Okay," I said. I took a deep breath and decided not to look at her. "Now, what do you say we take my uncle Roger's bicycle? We can get across the park faster. But first I'm going to leave a note for Aunt Bridget." I took down her note and scribbled, "Gone to Heliotrope Café to find Otto Pettingill. W." Then I pinned it back on to Flora's chest. "I don't think that's any weirder than her notes to me."

Uncle Roger's bike was in the shed in the back of the apartment building. Aunt Bridget had shown it to me, saying I could use it anytime I wanted to. It was an old bike, that's for sure, a three-speed and pretty rusty. "It's better than nothing," I said.

We walked it across the street and then headed south through the park, Liesl balancing herself on the bar in front of me. All of a sudden we heard, "Hey, Willy!" My blood froze. Braking hard, I nearly sent us both flying. "Hey, Willy! Where the heck have you been, and what are you doing in that gorilla suit?" Gareth was standing on the grass next to the bike path.

I stared at him. "How the heck did you know it was me?"

"I'd know Roger McTaggart's bike anywhere. It's the most ancient thing in the park, except for Old Violet." Gareth tugged at his cap. "So who's your mate?"

Liesl whirled off the bike in a fury and began to attack Gareth. Gareth laughed. "Knock it off, Liesl." Then more seriously he said, "I'm really ticked at the two of you. I can't understand how you guys could so totally blow off the team. I mean, I don't even know why I'm standing here talking to you."

"Listen," I said, beginning to feel swimmy with sweat inside the gorilla suit. "You wouldn't have known it was me except for the bike, right? And you wouldn't have known it was Liesl except she was with me?"

"Right," said Gareth, running his tongue over his

braces. "Except for the bike, I wouldn't have looked twice. It's totally normal to see two gorillas riding on an ancient bike through the park. Do you know how soon we're playing the Sharks? Do you even care? It's probably the last game I'll ever play in Gill Park." He punched a fist into his glove and looked away.

"Listen, Gareth," I said. "There's a chance we can save the park, and then you can play a million more games and slaughter the Sharks a thousand times over, but you have to sit down and listen for a moment." I kicked out the old kickstand on the bike and led Gareth over to a bench.

"What are we doing?" Liesl asked.

"I'm just explaining everything to him," I said. "Sit down and relax for a minute."

"I'm not going to sit down. My butt is wicked sore from riding like that. Next time *you* sit there and I'll pedal."

"Do you even know how to ride a bike?" I asked doubtfully.

"Yes, I know how to ride a bike, Willy Wilson." She pulled her mask down, maybe so I could see her expression of fury. "Mr. Pettingill taught me himself."

"Put the mask back on," I said, slightly panicked.

"So are you two going to argue all day or are you going to let me in on what's happening?" Gareth asked.

Liesl slipped the mask back on and hovered in front of us while I told Gareth the story. He sat still while I talked—not a single freckle bounced. I don't think I had ever seen him be so still.

When I had finished, he sprang up from the bench. "Okay if I talk now?" he asked. I nodded. "I was going to run a strategy meeting with the team this afternoon," he said, looking at his watch. "But just this once I'm going to make a sacrifice. I think I should go to the café. With those gorilla suits on, you stick out like a Ping-Pong player on the pitcher's mound. Sooner or later they're going to figure it out and pick you up. It's safer for me to go."

I thought, *Wow, I should be relieved—grateful, even, for Gareth's offer,* but I was suddenly incredibly disappointed. It was *my* adventure—the first and only adventure of my whole life. And there was another thing. I wanted to meet Otto Pettingill myself. I wanted to see the king of Gill Park face-to-face.

eighteen

It was the park music that did it.
Growing up with it, listening to it all my life—
that's why I'm a musician now.

—*Dave Healy*

"No way," said Liesl, jumping into the conversation before I could say anything. "He was *my* guardian. He dumped me. I'm going to find him, and I'm going to give him a piece of my mind."

"If you get caught, Liesl, then the park gets sold," Gareth said. "Have you thought about that?"

"I'm going," said Liesl, hands on her gorilla hips. "You can wimp out, Willy Wilson, but I'm going."

"I don't think you realize how serious this is, Liesl," I said.

"Oooh, you both make me so mad. I'm going and you can't stop me."

She stomped off, and before we could stop her, she hopped on the bike—hopped because it was too big for her. She forgot to kick up the kickstand, though, so when she started to pedal, the stand caught and she tipped over, the bike falling on top of her.

"Liesl!" I yelled, running over to her.

I think in that moment Liesl became a real gorilla. With a sort of grunt, she swung the bike up, kicked up the kickstand, climbed on, and with her feet barely reaching the pedals, stormed off.

"Liesl!" I yelled. "Liesl! Come back here."

"Shut up, you idiot," said Gareth. He was bouncing from foot to foot, running his tongue across his braces. "You're screaming her name all over the place."

"She's the idiot," I groaned. "She's going to ruin everything."

"Willy, I think you should go after her. I even think you should be the one to go to the café."

"Are you serious?" I asked.

"Look, the fact that Liesl would even get on that bike with you in the first place is amazing. She never lets people get close to her. If I showed up at the café, she'd scream at me or do something really stupid."

I reached down inside the neck of the gorilla suit and scratched. It certainly was making me sweat and itch. I felt sorry for the Gorilla Rockettes or whoever it was who was going to dance in these things. I considered what Gareth had just said. As usual, he was probably right.

Gareth looked at his watch. "Call me when you get home. If you don't, I'll get my dad and come looking for you."

"Okay," I said weakly. So Gareth thought there was a possibility I might not get home. What could happen? The police could pick me up and what? But why would the police pick *me* up? No one was out looking for *me*.

"Well, good luck, Willy." Gareth slapped me on my gorilla back.

"Yup," I said.

I headed south. There was Old Violet on her bench. I had an urge to sit beside her and see if she'd say, "What a big gorilla you are, *ha!*"

I was becoming more and more nervous. Perfectly ordinary things like trash cans, benches, and trees looked sinister. As I passed the fountain, I saw the girl in pink smoking a cigarette and talking on a cell phone again. Maybe she'd been talking since the day before yesterday when I'd seen her. A bunch of boys in flip-flops and backpacks were clustered around her. I imagined the backpacks were full of drugs and knives. I didn't want to walk by them. On a bench, a man with long black hair in dreads was watching them, laughing. He scared me, too. Since coming to Aunt Bridget's and the park, I'd been more comfortable here than any other place I'd ever been—but now that old feeling of not belonging was creeping back, that old feeling that everyone else in the world was comfortable except for me, that I was an oddball, not even comfortable in my own skin.

Then I couldn't help laughing at myself. *In my own skin.* I looked down at my own skin. My skin was black and fuzzy. *A gorilla,* I thought, *is strong. It's hard to hurt a gorilla.*

I walked by the kids and they turned and stared at me and then they laughed.

"Hey, King Kong," the guy with the dreads called out.

I kept going, pretending I hadn't heard him, and imagined that the fountain lights were turned on. I stopped again and watched. I could see the colors inside my mind. Red, red, red, green, green, green, yellow, yellow, yellow, blue. I didn't know the Mozart sonata the fountain was supposed to be in time to, but I thought maybe Pachelbel's Canon might work with it. I hummed the tune inside myself. Yeah, that worked. And I felt calm and brave in that moment and completely in my own skin.

"Bye, King Kong," the guy called from the bench as I moved on. I waved. I waved to the kids and the girl in pink, too. I thought, *In another year or two, I'll be them. I'll be hanging around in the park and people will automatically be afraid of me because I'm a teenager.*

A policeman rode by on a bicycle. The kids moved together slightly and the man on the bench shifted. Seeing the cop shocked me into action. He was probably out looking for Liesl. If I didn't get going, there wouldn't *be* a park to hang out in.

When I finally reached the south side, I had to ask a bunch of people where the Heliotrope Café was. A man in baggy white pants with a pink bandanna around his head and an earring in his ear was standing in front of the café when I finally reached it. "You got a reservation?" he asked me. The fact that he was speaking to a gorilla didn't seem to bother him at all.

"I'm supposed to meet my father here," I said. I pointed to a poster that said, DAVE HEALY TONITE underneath a guy in a turtleneck playing a guitar. "He's playing tonight and he said to meet him here."

"Your dad's Dave Healy? Cool," said the man and he let me walk by him. "You'll find him downstairs."

Inside, the café was crammed with people. They sat around tables or on benches along the sides or perched on stools at the bar at the back. At the front, an old guy sat playing the piano on a stage that was really just a slightly raised platform. No one was paying much attention to him. Probably he was just playing until Dave Healy came on.

People laughed and pointed at me as I scanned the crowd looking for Liesl. Where the heck was she?

"Excuse me," I asked a couple at a table. "Did you see another gorilla walk in here?"

The guy laughed and said, "Sorry, not today, but that's a great outfit you've got on."

A knot began forming in the pit of my stomach. Where was she? The baggy-pants guy had said I would find Dave Healy downstairs. That meant there was a downstairs. Well, maybe that's where Liesl was. I found the stairs, and as I was going down them, another couple stopped me. "What's this gorilla stuff made of?" the man wanted to know.

"I don't know," I said.

"It's synthetic," said the woman, petting the fur on my arm.

"It'd be great to have hair all over you like that," said the man. "No need for clothes."

"Except then people would shave it or dye it and get body permanents," said the woman, laughing.

Right then and there I decided to ditch the gorilla suit. It was so hot, and I was way too conspicuous with it on. I found a bathroom and peeled it off. Phew. What a relief to be out of that hot, sweaty, sticky, itchy thing. The real hair on my arms tingled in the air. I stuffed the suit and the mask into a ball and, holding them under my arm, went out into the hallway. I poked my head into a half open door and there was Dave Healy, looking older than he did in his poster. A couple of other people were with him, sitting at a table, eating.

"Did you see a gorilla come in here?" I asked. "Or a girl?"

"No gorillas and no girls," said Dave Healy with a smile.

I trudged back upstairs. Maybe Liesl had been sitting up there in that room all along but it had been too crowded to see her. She would have seen me come in, though, wouldn't she? And what about Otto Pettingill? Where was he? And how was I going to be able to recognize him? Liesl had started to draw him that one time in the park—a bald guy with a big nose and a pointed beard.

I found a space to sit at the end of a bench in a dark corner. I needed to sit still for a minute and think about what to do. The piano music drifted through the chatter and laughter of the people, through the clink of glasses and the scraping of forks on plates. It reminded me of Otto Pettingill's music, the way it wove through all the sounds. The way that phrase slid down the scale, I could perfectly picture that day I walked back from playing baseball with Gareth on the way to Rosa's Market. . . . I could see the blue of the sky, feel the breeze on my face, smell the popcorn and cotton candy. I remembered how good I'd felt walking with Gareth, feeling like Gareth was going to be a friend. . . .

I looked once more at the man playing the piano. He was going bald and he had a big nose and a pointy beard. I knew at that moment that without a doubt I had found Otto Pettingill.

nineteen

I'm not as fond of Rollie
as I was of his father—
he's a bit of a cold fish—but I'm glad
I've been able to keep my affairs in the family.

—*Otto Pettingill*

I drew in a deep breath and sat tight. Okay. I would sit there for a minute and not do anything. Just stare at the guy. He wasn't completely bald; there were a few strands of gray hair matted to his scalp. He didn't seem very tall, although it was hard to tell, but his face was thin and very wrinkled, with high, hollow cheekbones, and sad, sad, sad.

I got up and moved over to the edge of the platform. Baggy Pants passed me a few times without bugging me to move, so I stayed. Otto Pettingill came to the end of his piece. He stretched his arms and then his fingers, and then sat still on the piano stool and looked out at the crowd with a sad smile. Then he started to cough. It was a long, hacky cough, and it made me wonder if he was all right. When he finally stopped, he sighed and slid off the stool and began to walk off the platform.

He saw me staring at him. "I expect you're waiting for the real thing," he said. "He should be coming up any moment now."

I stood up and touched Mr. Pettingill's arm. He had that stingy smell about him, the way people do who smoke a lot. "I think *you're* the real thing," I said.

"What? Why, thank you," Mr. Pettingill said, his face lighting up with his smile. His voice had a smoky choke to it. "I'm astonished to find that anyone was listening—a boy at that," he said, taking me in. His eyes were surprising—younger than the rest of him, not cloudy or vague; you could see he noticed things.

He began to thread his way through tables to the back of the room. "Listen," I said, grabbing his arm, the worry about Liesl driving me to be bold. "I like your music and miss it. Why did you stop playing for the park?"

Mr. Pettingill turned and stared at me. "What did you say?"

"I know who you are," I whispered. "And there's a problem with Liesl Summer. The family she was supposed to go and live with. There's a problem," I had to raise my voice at the end because Dave Healy was coming into the room and the crowd had begun to whistle and clap.

What color there had been seemed to drain out of Mr. Pettingill's face. "Let's get out of here," he said.

He turned around and pushed me out of the café. It was a warm night, but cooler than in the café, and I felt as if I could breathe better outside. We walked a few feet away into the parking lot of a bank, where it was pretty quiet. Mr. Pettingill brought out a pack of cigarettes and lit one with a shaking hand. He inhaled and then breathed out the smoke.

"Now," Mr. Pettingill said in his choky voice. "First things first. Who are you?"

I swallowed hard. "My name is Willy Wilson. I—I'm visiting my aunt. She's Bridget McTaggart. She—she makes costumes."

Mr. Pettingill frowned. "Bridget McTaggart . . . Oh, yes, I know who she is. Her husband died recently—tragedy—talented fellow."

"Talented?" I asked uncertainly.

"He was a violinist, a very promising one . . ."

My mouth fell open. "He was a *violinist?*" Why didn't I know that? That night, when I had played the violin and Aunt Bridget had leaned against the door with tears in her eyes . . . but she had never said . . . did she think I knew? I should have known. I wished Dad and Aunt Bridget had gotten along. I wished my parents hadn't been so stuck-up about them. I would have known Uncle Roger better. *He* could have taught me the violin . . .

"All right, now for the next question," Mr. Pettingill said, breaking into my thoughts. He tapped the ash off his cigarette. "Just what have *you* to do with Liesl Summer?"

I took a breath. "I'm . . . I'm her friend," I said.

Mr. Pettingill exploded. "Friend! That's a new one!"

"I can't exactly explain it," I said. "I don't really know her, but there's something about her—anyhow," I said, worried again, and impatient. "I was there when Mr. Brookings came over and told her you had decided she should live with a family and go to school. She sure was happy about the idea of going to school," I added.

Mr. Pettingill screwed up his face. He looked like I had kicked him. "School," he said. "The long, dark hours of boredom . . . and she would choose that? Go on."

"So she went with them. But they were the wrong kind of people for her. They were really neat and clean and rich and I think they thought they could just clean her up and cut her hair and make her be what they wanted."

Mr. Pettingill coughed. There were shadows under his dark eyes. He threw the cigarette down and crushed it under the heel of his shoe.

"And then the next thing we knew, the music stopped and you were selling the park." I kicked my foot against the pavement. "How come?" I couldn't quite believe I was talking to Otto Pettingill like this, the most powerful man in the city of Gloria. But then he *wasn't* the most powerful man in Gloria: Roland Brookings and Frank Featherstone had outsmarted him.

"Roland Brookings gave me the impression that people didn't seem to care for it anymore," said Mr. Pettingill. "It was filling up with trash, there was broken glass where people should have been able to sit on the grass. I decided I'd test 'em—offer it up for sale and give 'em a few days to make some sort of protest. Tonight at midnight's the deadline," he said, looking at his watch. "If they seemed to care, I wouldn't sell it. If they let it all go without a murmur—well, then I have my answer. Looks as if I do have my answer. Rollie was supposed to contact me if there was a protest."

People walked by us on the street, laughing. Mr. Pettingill turned his head and looked at them sadly, as if they were the people who had let him down.

"But Mr. Pettingill, the people *did* protest. Mitch Bloom collected hundreds of names. Gareth Pugh and I even collected a lot. But your lawyer took all the petitions and never told you." I took a deep breath. "And then he went in with this guy called Frank Featherstone—" Mr. Pettingill put a hand against his heart and stood absolutely still, so still and silent I was scared. Was he having a heart attack? I was half afraid to go on. "Your lawyer made a deal to buy the park with Frank Featherstone. But Liesl complicated things because they think Liesl will come crying to you, and you'll come out of hiding or whatever it is that you're doing, and then you'll find out he let you down, and you'll find out what else he's been up to, before the deal can go through. They're buying the park so they can turn it into a *mall*." I was so mad I kicked the side of the bank.

Mr. Pettingill leaned against the wall and shielded his eyes with his hand. "Perfidy," he said in a low voice. "Treachery."

"And she was supposed to be at the café, looking for you, and she isn't, and I think they may have her, and Mr. Brookings was saying things like he was going to put her in a foster home."

Mr. Pettingill's hand came down abruptly. His eyes were bright now, and glittery. He was smiling from ear to ear. The wrinkles on his face curved up. He didn't look like a man who was having a heart attack. He took out another cigarette and lit it. "Well," he said. "Now that I know the worst, I am going to cook his goose. And you, Willy Wilson," he said, waving the cigarette at me, "may have the honor of being my fellow chef. Are you ready to pay a visit to Roland N. Brookings Jr.?"

"I—yes," I said.

"A jaunt across the park. Come along." He threw his shoulders back and started to walk. He didn't walk fast and he seemed to get winded easily—those stupid cigarettes he smoked—so it wasn't difficult to keep up with him.

We walked through the gates of his park. "I'm worried about Liesl," I said. "And I'm also worried—"

"About what, dear boy?"

"I had this idea you were the most powerful man in Gloria, but Mr. Brookings fooled you. I—"

"You're afraid of him," said Mr. Pettingill, turning to look at me. "You're afraid of what he might do when we show up on his doorstep. But not to worry,

Willy, my boy. I've taken a slight vacation is all—a bit of depression. But you have revived my spirits. I can out-fool Rollie Brookings any day of the year. But, here's an idea." Mr. Pettingill stopped and looked at me thoughtfully. A man and a woman walking a dog strolled by. The man had a big bunch of keys swinging from his belt, and they made a jangling noise as he walked.

"Evening," said the man, nodding to us.

"Beautiful evening," said Mr. Pettingill.

"It's always beautiful at this time of the night in the park," said the woman. "Everything's soft in the evening light, and all the flowers Mitch Bloom's planted smell so good in the night air, and the fountain's so pretty. . . ."

We all turned to look. There it was in the center of everything, red, red, red, green, green, green, yellow, yellow, yellow, blue, real colors now, one fading into another. I tried to catch the moment it happened but I couldn't, and it was a bit windy, so the watery plumes were more feathery than usual.

"And best of all, it's always so safe. Isn't it a shame that all this will be gone?" said the woman. "What is Otto Pettingill thinking of?"

"I told you, Sylvia," said the man, jangling his keys. "He sold out. The money was too good—prime property in the middle of the city. They all do in the end, you know."

The couple and the dog moved on. We could hear the keys jangling for quite a while. Mr. Pettingill's face was lit up like a big happy moon.

"I told you," I said.

"You told me," he said. He threw down his cigarette and rubbed his hands together. "Now for that thought I had. Roland actually laid eyes on you, did he not?"

"Yes—in his office. I ended up hiding behind a chair and I heard everything Mr. Brookings and Mr. Featherstone talked about."

"You hid behind a chair? Why, Willy, I'm shocked—and pleased, considering the circumstances."

"But Liesl came in and shouted out my name and we ran out of there. I don't know how well he saw me, but he'd already met me once before, in the park, when he told Liesl she was being adopted. He might recognize me if he saw me again."

"Well, it would be better if, when he comes to the door, he doesn't recognize you. I want to cook his goose slowly."

"So you don't want me to go with you?" I asked. I didn't know if I was relieved or disappointed.

"Yes, yes, dear boy, I do, I do. What fun I'm going to have, and you've been so splendidly courageous, I want you to share in the fun—and I'm sure you'll prove yourself resourceful and useful. We shall drop in on your aunt Bridget and she will figure out how to disguise you so that you can come with me to cook a goose without being recognized."

twenty

Of all the instruments
I ever heard Otto Pettingill play,
I liked hearing him play the violin the best.
—Roger McTaggart

"Willy!" Aunt Bridget rushed to the door as we came in. "It was getting late and I was beginning to worry."

A terrible realization struck me as I looked at her. "Aunt Bridget," I blurted out, "Liesl and I borrowed two gorilla suits because we had to be disguised and I left mine at the café, and I don't know where the other one is because I don't know where Liesl is. I'm so sorry—I'll go back and get it tomorrow, and Uncle Roger's bike, Liesl had that too—and Aunt Bridget, this is Mr. Pettingill."

Aunt Bridget's eyebrows shot right up and she stared like a little kid at Mr. Pettingill for a moment before she put out her hand and said, "Well, hello. Willy left me a note saying he was going to find you!"

"And, by God, he has! A resourceful boy, in all sorts of ways. You must be proud to have him as your nephew," said Mr. Pettingill, taking her hand in his. "You have quite a reputation in the park," he added. "You are known far and wide for the work you do. And I am sorry for your loss. Your Roger was a talented musician."

"Aunt Bridget, you never told me," I burst in again. "I didn't know Uncle Roger played the violin."

Aunt Bridget's eyes widened. "My goodness," she said. "And I thought, somehow, you played the violin because of him."

"I do now," I said.

"A violinist, eh?" said Mr. Pettingill, looking at me. He coughed for a long moment and I held my breath, waiting for him to get through it. Aunt Bridget turned away and busied herself with the gorillas. I went over and helped her. It seemed rude to stare at him while he was coughing, but it also seemed strange to pretend it wasn't happening. There was a rack in the living room now where the finished gorilla suits hung; the heads were stacked to one side.

"Ah, that's done with," Mr. Pettingill said finally. He leaned against a chair, gasping slightly.

"Can I get you a glass of water?" Aunt Bridget asked. "And please do sit down."

"Lovely," said Mr. Pettingill. He sat in a chair and

stroked his beard, looking around the room with interest. "Not your average home," he said as Aunt Bridget handed him the glass.

"I do apologize for the mess," she said with an embarrassed smile. "I have an order for thirty gorillas."

I bit my lip. Poor Aunt Bridget. All that work, and Liesl and I had just made it worse.

"Thirty gorillas!" Mr. Pettingill began to laugh his choky laugh and I thought he was going to go into another long cough again, but this time he seemed able to stop himself. "Now then, you mustn't apologize for being creative, and it is just your particular form of creativity that has brought us here." Aunt Bridget pushed back her hair and raised her eyebrows again. "Your nephew happened upon a plot being hatched by my attorney and another accomplice in greed. They want to turn *my* park into a mall! My attorney also may very likely have my ward Miss Liesl Summer under lock and key. Now it is my wish to confront said attorney, bringing your boy along with me, but it would be provident to disguise the boy, who, having inveigled himself into my attorney's office and made himself a nuisance, does not wish to be recognized."

Aunt Bridget turned to look at me. She frowned, making clicking sounds with her tongue against her teeth. "Well," she finally said. "The best way to disguise yourself is to change the color of your hair. You'd be surprised how that changes a person. How'd you like to be a redhead, Willy? I just happen to have some dye on hand. We did *Anne of Green Gables* this winter and the girl who played Anne had hair about the same color as yours and it worked just fine on her. And don't worry, it won't last that long. It'll be mostly gone before your mother sees it and has a heart attack. A very pretty auburn it'll come out, actually, not red at all. And we'll top it off with a pair of spectacles, I think, and a crisply ironed shirt and tie."

"It sounds like a recipe," I said. Aunt Bridget put back her head and laughed. "A recipe for cooking goose," I added.

Mr. Pettingill chuckled, now, too. It was very satisfying, this business of making people laugh—I liked it a lot.

While I stuck my head over the kitchen sink and Aunt Bridget poured the dye into my hair, Mr. Pettingill sat at the kitchen table. He was looking at newspapers from the last few days and he sat clucking and fuming. "Treason," he moaned. "Insurrection. Absolute idiocy."

When Aunt Bridget finally finished with me, I stared at myself in the mirror and could hardly believe what I saw. I looked like the preppiest kid in my school.

"What do you think?" Aunt Bridget asked.

"I actually think my parents would like me like this," I said, straightening the tie the way my dad always did. "I need a pen for my pocket."

"Right," said Aunt Bridget, finding one.

"You look dashing," Mr. Pettingill said approvingly. "By what name shall I address you?"

"How about Patrick?" Aunt Bridget suggested. "Patrick Bentley."

"Perfect," said Mr. Pettingill. "Now, then, thank you so much, Mrs. McTaggart; and Patrick, let us be on our way. A taxi, I think, for this last leg of the journey. I'm feeling a bit weary, and I must be at my best for this goose cooking."

Our taxi coasted through the streets; there wasn't much traffic now. We passed tall dark trees—they seemed like shadows, not like solid things, and I thought about night and how there's no color in the night, but wondered if things like leaves are still green even when you can't see the green, and that made me think of the thing they always ask you—if a tree falls in a forest and no one is around to hear it, does it still make a sound? And that made me wonder about taste—I mean, if no one ever ate a lemon, would it be sour? Or, if you have notes on a page, and no one ever played the notes, would it be music? And then my mind jumped to Mr. P. Would Mr. P., if he saved his park, play his music again?

Mr. P. said, "You're very quiet, Willy, my boy. Are you feeling nervous about our escapade?"

"I'm wondering if you'll go back to playing your music," I said.

"Would you like me to?" he asked.

"Yes," I said. I put all my heart into that yes.

"Hmmm," said Mr. P. I could see him stroking his beard and looking at me. "How many other people do you think feel this way about my music?"

"Aunt Bridget does," I said. "She says the music helps her remember Uncle Roger."

"Well, that's two in the city of Gloria," said Mr. P.

"But don't you think it presumptuous to foist my particular taste on other people—"

"It's your park . . ."

"But that has perhaps been the problem, that they don't feel as if it belongs to them."

"You could have a couple of days a week where you invite other people to play," I said. "Each person could get an hour or something. You could have a sign-up sheet."

"Ha!" said Mr. P. "Ha, ha, ha!" He thumped my knee with his hand. "What an idea, my boy, what an idea!"

I wasn't sure what he meant. Did he like it or not? I was about to ask him when the taxi stopped. "Well, Willy, and just who is Patrick Bentley? When I present you to Mr. Brookings, I need to have a good story."

"I could be another orphan who has to be placed with a family," I said.

"My word, you are just full of brilliant ideas tonight," he said, leaning forward to pay the cab driver. He opened the door. "What sort of family would you like to live with?" he asked.

I thought for a moment. Then I said, "Yours."

He looked startled. "Mine?" The coughing started and he thumped on his chest. "Oh, be quiet," he told himself.

"You could adopt me," I said. "I mean for real. I could live in Liesl's old apartment. Belle Vera could take care of me and I wouldn't have to go to school and I could pick out my own clothes and my own food. I could spend all day learning how to play the violin until I am as good as Uncle Roger was. I bet Liesl draws as good as she does because she didn't have other useless stuff distracting her."

Mr. Pettingill looked at me and smiled. "I like to think so," he said. "But not all people think that is a good thing. And you do have parents, don't you?"

"I'm not the right kind of person for them."

"Perhaps they're not the right kind for you."

"Well, yeah. It's mutual."

"Even so, they might have some regrets if you told them you were being adopted by someone else."

"Mom would be a little concerned at first, but my dad would reassure her that it was for the best."

Mr. P. shook his head. "Well, they may grow up and learn to appreciate you. They ought to, anyway, a fine boy like you. Be patient, give them a chance. Most parents do grow up, you know. Mine did, but it took them a while." He choked a little as he finished speaking.

I held my breath, hoping he wouldn't go into one of his long coughs. I felt a sort of fury rising from the pit of my stomach. "Mr. P.," I said, "why don't you quit smoking?"

"Ah, dear boy, it's one of the few pleasures left to me."

"No, it's *not!*" I felt myself grow hot. I was so angry I wanted to kick him. I wanted to throw a Liesl tantrum. "You have a whole park and a fountain and Liesl to give you pleasure. What are you talking about?"

Mr. P. patted my shoulder. "And a young man like you. Well, I confess, you do give me hope—but I shall not have a park unless we get moving now." He glanced at his watch. "Good God, we only have thirty-five minutes to cook this goose. Cheer up, Willy, I'm not dead yet."

I slowly followed him into the lobby of the apartment building where Roland N. Brookings Jr. lived, still shaking slightly from anger. I couldn't look at Mr. P. as we rode up in the elevator.

When Mr. Brookings answered the doorbell and saw Mr. Pettingill, he looked as if he wanted to slam the door in his face. I was standing behind Mr. P., so he couldn't see me too well. I could feel my stomach churning as I watched Mr. Brookings' face. It pulled one way with surprise, and then the other with fear. In the end, it came out blank.

"Well," he said finally. "What a surprise." Then the blankness gave way to a crocodile smile, his teeth all sharp and pointy. "It's rather late, but do come in."

"I've brought a young man with me." Mr. P. said as we stepped into the apartment. Mr. Brookings looked at me curiously and I tried not to squirm. "I'd like you to meet Patrick Bentley. He's a young man in need of a home, and as you've done so well by Liesl Summer, I thought you could do something for this boy."

Mr. Brookings seemed to relax slightly. "By all means," he said. "Delighted to meet you, Patrick." He took my hand and gave it a clammy shake. He flashed his best crocodile smile at me. My legs were trembling, waiting for the moment of recognition, but he seemed to look *through* me, not really *at* me.

"Not a problem, Otto. A nice-looking boy. Perhaps easier to place than Liesl. Of course, she is a most interesting child. Ahem. Happy to help out. Do sit down, Patrick, make yourself comfortable."

Mr. Pettingill and I sat down on a leather couch. I took a breath and looked around. I remembered now Mr. Brookings saying, "What people really want is *things*."

Well, there seemed to be a lot of things in his apartment—chairs and desks and paintings with gold frames and little statues and dogs made out of china and boxes with scrolly decorations and sofas and rugs and clocks and bowls and lamps and a rack with all different kinds of pipes, the kind you smoke, and another rack with bottle openers, and a big frame of butterflies arranged by colors. It all smelled of furniture polish, and there was a big grandfather clock, dark and made of heavy wood in one corner.

Mr. Brookings sat in an armchair opposite us. It was leather, too, with little brass knobby things outlining the shape of it. "Your need to find a place for the young man must be rather urgent for you to come see me so late," he said, casting a glance at the clock.

"Yes," said Mr. P. "It *is* late." He crossed his legs, "But not *too* late, Rollie, I'm glad to say. You don't seem to be in bed asleep, at any rate."

"The young man is your only reason for your visit?"

"Well," said Mr. P., "it's close to the hour of midnight, is it not?"

"Yes it is," said Mr. B., glancing at the clock again.

"And at midnight, the time I allotted for protest runs out."

"I believe you mentioned something of the sort," Mr. Brookings said, inspecting his nails.

"I know we left it that you would contact me, but I came rather hoping you'd heard something—any little thing."

Mr. Brookings leaned forward, his arms on his legs, and I could see his freckly hands trembling slightly, just like my legs. He shook his head. "I'm sorry, Otto," he said with a sigh. "I'm truly sorry. There doesn't seem to have been more than a murmur. Mitch Bloom, he did seem upset—it has more to do with his dwelling, I suppose—"

Mr. P. slapped a hand against his forehead. "Good God!" he said. "Of course. I never thought about his living situation. Poor fellow!"

"I'm sure you can make some sort of arrangement for him," Mr. Brookings said smoothly. "But, as you suspected, the people do not seem to care very much whether they have a park or not."

"Ah," said Mr. P. "Perhaps, after all, it is for the best."

Mr. Brookings raised his eyebrow. "Really, Otto," he said. "I'm pleased to hear you say so."

"Pleased, are you, Rollie? What a curious thing for you to say. Why on earth should you be pleased?"

"Pleased you are facing the loss so realistically," said Mr. Brookings. He brought his hands together and then began squeezing them, first one then the other.

"I am a realist," said Mr. Pettingill.

"Really?" the king of snorts snorted, and then quickly cleared his throat to cover up. "Really," he said again in fake agreement.

"If you think a dreamer cannot also be a realist, you are mistaken, Roland," said Mr. Pettingill. Then he shut his eyes and leaned back against the couch. "The most dangerous characteristic of dreamers, though, is that they tend to trust where they should not trust."

Mr. Brookings frowned. "Frankly, Otto, I'm not sure I follow you."

"Frankly Featherstone," Mr. Pettingill said softly, opening his eyes slightly.

"What?" Mr. Brookings sat up straight as if he'd been pricked.

"I said, *frankly,* I know," said Mr. Pettingill, opening his eyes all the way and leaning forward. "Well, in any case, I also came here to see if you could put me in touch with the family you found for Liesl." The grandfather clock ticked loudly, sounding like Brookings' heart, I thought. *Tick tick tick. He's going to explode in a minute.* "I know you've been so competent and careful and I am eager to meet them."

Mr. Brookings' eyes darted from Mr. P. to the hallway leading out from his living room. And in that moment there was a sound of someone pounding on a door.

"Let me out, you slimy creep! You better let me out! If you don't I'm going to kick down your stupid door!"

Mr. Brookings went white and Mr. P. and I looked at each other and grinned. "Why, Rollie," said Mr. P. "I recognize those lovely, lilting tones. Why, you sly dog, why didn't you tell me? You took the child in yourself! What an idea! How very, very kind of you!"

twenty-one

Whoever said beauty can't be bought
was wrong.
—*Roland N. Brookings Jr.*

The grandfather clock ticked in the silence, and then there was more commotion from down the hall. *"Let me out!"*

Mr. Brookings raised a pudgy finger to his mouth and began to chew the skin around the nail.

"It was, as I said, very kind of you to take the child in," said Mr. P. "What an ingenious solution. I know you are a trustee of the East Park Day School. But are you sure you are quite up to it?"

"I—I didn't!" Mr. Brookings sputtered. "She—unfortunately—in spite of careful research—she did not like the family I placed her with."

"Oh," said Mr. P. He raised his arms in surprise. "Well, perhaps I could be of some help. We've always gotten along rather well—kindred souls in a way. Perhaps I could coax her into staying with . . . whoever it was?"

"I'm not sure they'll have her back. She was very difficult. But she's in the back bedroom. I'll go and get her. She may . . . she may say some things about me—she has been very upset."

"Don't give it another thought," said Mr. P. cheerfully. "I understand the volatile nature of the girl."

Mr. Brookings rushed out of the room. As soon as he was gone, Mr. P. leaped up, rubbing his hands together. "I have it all worked out, Willy. It's perfect, it really is."

"Don't you touch me, you slimy creep! I'll spit in your face if you come near me."

Mr. P. made a face and shrugged. "Oh dear," he murmured. "Is this the Frankenstein I have created?"

"She's not always like this," I reassured him. And then I thought of something. "Oh my gosh, she'll recognize me and she'll make a big scene."

"We'll handle it," Mr. P. said calmly. "We can handle anything, Willy, my boy." Wheezing slightly, he moved toward the hall. "Hold on, Rollie," he called hoarsely. "I'm coming in!" He put up a hand to shield his face as if he were about to plunge into a tornado, then moved quickly down the hall.

In a moment, Mr. Brookings came back in. His face was red and he was fuming. My heart sank.

He'd recognize me now for sure, with no one else in the room to look at, but he turned his back on me and walked over to his window and stared out. I looked out, too. There, far below us, in the center of the park, the fountain bloomed like a flower.

Red, red, red, green, green, green, yellow, yellow, yellow, blue . . . My heart seemed to slow to its rhythm and I calmed down.

Loud squeals came from the hallway. Turning slightly, Brookings narrowed his icy eyes. "Now what?" he grumbled.

Mr. P. came striding back into the room, followed by Liesl. My heart bumped to see her. She was all right. She was her old self The yellow dress was rumpled now and no longer looked clean, and that was so much better. Her short hair even managed to look messy. The blue vein on the bridge of her nose blazed, but for once her eyes were shining and there was a big grin on her face. She took one look at me and actually winked. A very exaggerated wink. I was afraid I might start to laugh, but Mr. P. caught my eye and shook his head. Mr. Snort Brookings had turned from the window and was standing with his arms crossed against his chest.

"We've solved the adoption problem," Mr. P. said breezily.

"Have you?" Mr. B. asked heavily.

"She tells me Mitch Bloom has expressed an interest in her living with him."

"Has he?" asked Mr. B. cheerfully. He relaxed his

arms and seemed to take a breath. "That is . . . that is a *fabulous* solution."

"One that I wish I had thought of myself," said Mr. P. "Instead of delegating such an important decision—"

"Now don't blame yourself, Otto—this has not been an easy time for you." Mr. B. took a step toward him.

Liesl curled her lip and snarled. Mr. P. put a hand on her shoulder. "Easy, girl, easy," he said.

Mr. Snort turned away in disgust. "She's like a dog! A little mad dog!"

"Easy, sir, easy," said Mr. P. warningly. "This is my pride and joy you are talking about."

Mr. Brookings turned his head slightly, but I could see him rolling his eyes. "And what about school?" he asked Liesl. "You've lost your chance with the East Park Day School—about the only chance you had, I would have thought."

Liesl raised her chin in the air. *"Je vais étudier avec Madame."*

Mr. Brookings looked at her blankly. Mr. P. smiled.

"I have told her she may live with Mitch Bloom on the condition that she allow Madame Belle Vera to be her teacher," said Mr. P. "She must attend classes with Madame every day until she can be integrated into a school."

Mr. Brookings shrugged. "All right," he said. "Very good. All's well that ends well. And now, Otto, it is rather late, wouldn't you agree? Perhaps we could tackle the boy's future when we are all feeling a little fresher?" He nodded in my direction.

"Actually, Rollie, this night I have learned my lesson. I shall take care of the boy's future myself."

"Well, that *is* fabulous," said Mr. Brookings. "We'll call it a day, then, shall we?" He extended a hand toward me. "So nice to have met you . . . I'm sorry, I've forgotten—"

"Patrick," I said, standing and shaking his hand firmly.

"It might, you know, Rollie, serve you to remember names and faces—can one go to school for that sort of thing, do you think? Take a class called Noticing People, Paying Attention to Others. Maybe there's an evening course called Familiar Faces at the community college. And I've already settled the question of Patrick. I am going to adopt him."

"You?" All three of us—Mr. Brookings, Liesl, and I—said it at the same time.

Mr. P. came over to me and put his arm around me. "Patrick's a lad after me own heart," he said, sounding Irish. He looked down at me, beaming. I looked back up at him, not quite understanding what he was up to.

"Sounds great to me," I said. "It's just what I wanted."

"And I thought," Mr. P. went on, "I'd begin fatherhood by giving my son an allowance. I can do that right now, don't you think, Roland?"

Mr. Brookings frowned. "I don't see why not," he said. By now I couldn't help feeling a little sorry for the guy. He had blue circles under his eyes.

"For this week I thought I'd give him this amount." Patting me on the back, Mr. P. brought down his arm, reached into his pocket, and pulled out a checkbook and fountain pen. He opened the checkbook and, propping it against my back, wrote something in it. Then he tore out the check with a flourish. He handed it to Mr. Brookings. "What do you think, Rollie?" he asked. "Do you think this is enough for a boy his age?"

The check trembled in Mr. B's hand. He was staring at it in disbelief. "But this check is for millions of dollars," he said.

"More than what even you and Frank Featherstone could possibly put together?" asked Mr. P.

Mr. B. didn't answer. He didn't even snort. The circles under his eyes turned even bluer in his white face.

With two long fingers, Mr. P. plucked the check from Mr. B.'s pudgy ones and handed it to me. "What would you like to buy with your allowance, son?" Mr. P. asked, turning to me.

I took a breath. There was a second of silence, the second of silence between the loud ticks of that clock. And when I spoke, my words came out at the same moment the clock began to chime midnight. I whispered hoarsely, "I would like to buy the park."

"Speak up," said Mr. P. "I don't think Rollie could quite hear you."

"The park," I said again, raising my voice. I waved the check in the air. I yelled. *"I would like to buy the park!"* And Liesl, who had been quiet and still all this time but had been sort of quivering like a dog that's been tied up too long, suddenly began racing around the apartment, squealing, "That's cool, Willy Wilson, that's cool."

"Willy Wilson!" Mr. Brookings finally realized who I was. He sank into his leather couch and didn't even say anything when Liesl's arm caught a china dog and sent it smashing to the floor.

twenty-two

I was so hyper when I was a kid,
no one could believe that I liked playing
the violin. What they didn't understand
was that there isn't a better feeling
than taking all that energy and
pulling it across a set of violin strings
and making it come out as beautiful music.
—*Roger McTaggart*

It was almost one o'clock in the morning by the time
Liesl and I walked up the creaky stairs to Aunt Bridget's apartment. Mr. P. had ridden home with us in a
taxi and then had gone on his way. Aunt Bridget
was still up, sitting in a chair in the living room,
reading a book. I think it was one of the only times I

had seen her doing something besides working on the gorillas.

"Well!" she exclaimed. "How'd it go? I couldn't sleep without knowing the outcome."

First Liesl told her she had lost the gorilla suit and Uncle Roger's bike. She said she'd been chased by a cop and she'd left both the suit and the bike under a tree. "I'm really, really sorry," she said. "Maybe we can find them. Maybe they're still there."

"I'm just glad you're okay," said Aunt Bridget. "Now tell me the rest of it."

Liesl and I told her the whole story, acting it out as we went along. I played Mr. Pettingill and Liesl played Mr. Brookings. Liesl imitated him so well it was both funny and creepy. Aunt Bridget sat watching, her eyes dancing, her hand over her mouth. When we got to the part where Mr. P. handed me a check and I said I wanted to buy the park, she clapped.

"Bravo! Bravo!" she cried. "What an ending! What a drama! And what did Mr. Brookings do then?"

"He started blubbering about how he hadn't meant to do any harm, but Mr. P. told him to keep his trapola shut or little bugs would fly in and buzz around inside that stupid skull of his," said Liesl.

"He didn't exactly say that," I said.

"In any case," Aunt Bridget said, "this calls for a celebration. Hot chocolate for all!"

She got up and went to the kitchen and we followed her. She pulled a bag of miniature marshmallows out of a cupboard. "These are a little stale," she said, banging the bag against the counter. "Hard as rocks, but they'll soften up. I think they've been around for a long time, but it's been a while since I've had a reason to celebrate."

After she'd made the hot chocolate, she floated about fifty little marshmallows in the top of each mug, and I had to admit as I sat in the kitchen with Aunt Bridget and Liesl, I couldn't remember a time in my life when I had been happier. Liesl gradually grew a marshmallow mustache and that made me feel even happier. She was the same old mess. And she was safe. I shuddered at the thought of her being sent to a foster home or orphanage or wherever Brookings was going to put her.

"And you get to go to school, Liesl," Aunt Bridget said.

Liesl nodded. "But first Belle Vera has to teach me stuff."

"Will you mind?" I asked. "Being taught by her, I mean?"

"Course not," she said. "Why should I?"

"Thought you might, that's all. I've heard you say some pretty mean things about her."

Liesl looked irritated. That was a good sign, too. She didn't seem so little and stepped on anymore. "For one thing," she said in a high-and-mighty tone of voice, "I'm not living with her anymore, and for another, I know she's going to be a good teacher. All these people who used to be her students still call her up and everything. I'm starting tomorrow."

"In that case," said Aunt Bridget, standing up with a yawn, "we'd all better go to sleep before it is tomorrow."

Even though I was so tired my head felt like lead, I sat on the bed in my secret cave bedroom and leaned on the windowsill. I turned my hands into a telescope and looked through it at the fountain. There it was, all its colors leaping in the blur of black that was the park. *It's safe,* I thought.

As I slid under the covers, a big solid weight jumped up on my chest, big and solid and purring. I stroked Sophie's soft fur. Life was good when a cat was breathing in your face. And tomorrow I'd get to see Mr. P.'s apartment and where the music came from. He'd invited me to come over to see it. Maybe I'd be there when he started playing music into the park again. I wondered what he'd choose to play— it'd have to be something triumphant and loud and brassy, like the trumpet music I'd heard my first day at Aunt Bridget's.

When I woke up, I could tell it was late from the way the sun streamed in the window. I sat up and listened. No music yet. I jumped out of bed. I wanted to get to Mr. P.'s as soon as possible, but then I heard Gareth's voice and figured it might be a while before I'd be able to escape.

Gareth was sitting at the kitchen table, a newspaper spread out on the table before him. A sleepy-looking Liesl sat at the table, too. "He woke me up with that loud voice of his," she complained.

"Your voice is a thousand times louder than mine," Gareth protested.

"Move the paper, will ya?" She had a huge bowl of cereal in front of her.

"So who's going to tell me what happened?" Gareth asked, pointing to the headlines with a spoon. GILL PARK NOT TO BE SOLD. OWNER OTTO HAS CHANGE OF HEART. PARK RENEWAL PLANS UNDER WAY.

"The park's not going to be sold," I said.

"I can see that," Gareth said impatiently. "But what happened with you guys?"

Once again, Liesl and I told the story. I thought we were becoming a regular comedy duo. Pretty soon we could take our routine on the road. When we finished, Gareth said, "So we can practice now. No more distractions. No more excuses."

"I have to help Bridget McTaggart make a new gorilla suit," said Liesl. "I left mine somewhere."

"I did too," I admitted.

"So we have to make two new ones."

"I have to go to Mr. Pettingill's," I said.

"Two o'clock," said Gareth, looking at his watch. "Be there."

I didn't even wait to eat breakfast or for Gareth to leave or to find out where Aunt Bridget might be. I took off down the stairs, raced across the street and into the park.

"You're safe!" I yelled out loud to the benches and the trees and the people who were walking by. I leaped into the air like a burst of water from the fountain. I leaped again and landed near Old Violet's bench. "You're safe!" I yelled at her. She stared at me and then opened her mouth so that I could see her perfect teeth, but I ran off before she could say anything. I wondered if she even knew what had almost happened to her.

I raced past Mitch Bloom's flower stand. There were banners all over it, brightly colored letters on them saying VICTORY. Belle Vera was standing with him. I waved to them but I didn't want to stop, because if I did, I'd have to tell them last night's story, too, and right then I just wanted to get to Mr. P.'s. I'd stop by and find them later.

Finally. East Thirteenth. Past the doorman. Into the elevator. The whole building had a lot of red in it, red carpets and red wallpaper along the hallway, and all these brass railings, which were shiny and polished; and the hallway and the elevator smelled like perfume and cigars. It looked rich and it smelled rich. It was hard to imagine Liesl living in this building.

Then I smelled cigarette smoke and knew I must be near Mr. P.'s door. And there it was. I rang the buzzer and a moment later he opened it with a big smile. "Willy!" he exclaimed. "I was beginning to wonder if you were going to show up." It was odd— in Mr. Brookings' apartment he had seemed to fill the living room, but in the doorway of his own place he looked smaller and older and more wrinkled.

"I'm sorry," I said. "I slept late."

"Well, come in, come in, better late than never."

I stepped through the door and then I just stared. It was a huge room, filled mostly with instruments. There were violins and a viola and a cello, a guitar and a banjo, a mandolin, a couple of saxophones and trumpets, an oboe and a clarinet, two flutes, a French horn, and a shiny black grand piano. The instruments were either hanging on the walls, which were white and bright, or resting on the floor, which was wooden and yellowish brown, with the grain of the wood all smooth and gleamy like a violin. Light poured in through a huge window that overlooked the park. I almost had to shade my eyes, there was so much gleaming of sun on wood and brass. And then I saw all this electronic equipment with millions of knobs and buttons and controls with wires and cables snaking out of them, attached to microphones hanging from the ceiling.

"So, you like my digs?" he asked. "I arranged for a sunny day today so you could see it at its best."

"It's amazing," I said. "Can you play all these instruments?"

He nodded. "Some better than others."

"How'd you learn?"

"I didn't go to school," he said with his choky laugh. "So I had plenty of time to learn."

"Do you have a favorite?"

He considered a moment. "I think it used to be the sax. Or the trumpet. You can communicate joy with those two almost better than anything else—you know, a wild kind of joy. The kind that makes you want to dance or do handsprings." Mr. P.'s wrinkles all curved up on his face like a million smiles, and his eyes were shining. He looked less shrively. "But I mostly play the piano or string instruments these days," he said. "It could be I'm mellowing with age, but more truthfully, it's difficult for me to play the wind instruments now, because, well, I get winded."

"You were playing the trumpet my first day here."

Mr. P. raised his eyebrows. "Is that right? Why, I remember, it wasn't that long ago. I hadn't played the trumpet in a long time, but everything seemed so perfect when I woke up. I felt the best I had in a long time. The sun was pouring in, the park looked all shiny and clean. I couldn't see the litter and the graffiti Roland was always going on about. The Trumpet Voluntary seemed like just the thing. Perhaps in some weird way I knew you had arrived, Willy, to bring hope back into my life."

I stretched a little and sat down on the shiny black piano bench. "So if you felt like that then, how come a few days later you were going to sell the park?"

"Well, as I told you, Roland had been giving me an earful. Day after day he'd been telling me how shabby things had gotten, how the people were bringing their boom boxes into the park to drown out my music."

I couldn't help smiling. It was funny to hear Mr. P. talk about boom boxes. "I think they like your music. They just like their music, too," I said.

"Such a reasonable lad," he said. "Where did you learn to be so reasonable?" I shrugged. "Born that way, I guess. And you also thought people might sign up to play their music into the park." This time I nodded.

"A man of few words," Mr. P. said, his wrinkles curving up again. "Well." He pulled on his beard and then took a violin down off the wall. "Here. This is your instrument, isn't it?"

"Mine?"

"I mean, it's what you play, isn't it?" He handed it to me. "Go on, let me hear you."

I felt the color rush to my face. If anybody else had asked me, I would have refused. I would have said, "I can't really play, I've only been taking lessons for a short time, I haven't practiced in a while." But they all felt like lame excuses. He'd just have to hear me and decide for himself.

"Is it . . . is it tuned?"

He took it from me and tuned it, quickly, professionally, and handed it back. The sun poured in that big window and onto the wide, varnished boards of the floor. A warm, friendly, almost bread-baking smell rose up from them. It was, I realized, a neat and clean room, but so different from the neat and clean of Mom's house. This was a room you wanted to stay in because it made you feel good and peaceful, instead of nervous about getting it dirty.

I took a breath and hoped I wouldn't play too badly. I pulled the bow across the strings. The only thing I really could play was that easy version of Pachelbel's Canon.

Mr. P. nodded as I finished. He didn't say it was good or bad, he just said, "Try holding your elbow like this," and he pushed my arm in closer to my body. Then he brought down another violin from the wall. "And hold the bow like this," he said, showing me. I copied him. "Yes, better," he said. "Now, play the piece again."

I played it again. He tapped my elbow with his bow when I forgot to hold my bow properly. He smiled when I finished. I knew it had sounded better the second time. "Now play with me," he said. "Do exactly what I do." He positioned his bow and began to play. I felt like a little kid going for a walk with someone who has much longer legs. It was hard to keep up, but it was fun, too. I tried to imitate the sweep of his arm and the confident way he played. My notes didn't exactly come out in the mellow way his did, but it made me feel like a pro. We played it twice like that.

"Stand here," he said when we'd finished. He used his bow to point to a spot on the floor. It was a worn spot, as if somebody had stood there a lot. I guessed it was where he stood to play most of his music. I went and planted myself there, somehow believing talent would seep up into my fingers just because my feet were where his feet had always been.

"Now," he said, "you will play the first music the people of the park will hear since it has been res- cued. It is only right that its rescuer should have the honor." He went over to one of the electronic con- traptions and flicked a switch, and there was a ping sound.

I stared at him with a beating heart.

"Now," he said, coming over to stand with me. "We'll play it three times. One, two, three, four." I lifted my bow and began to play. He joined me after the first four notes, and we played the Canon as a round. My arm trembled slightly and my hands were sweating. The second time through I began to relax, and I thought again about how my notes were like gold threads weaving together to form a ball that I was sending out to the park. I thought about how all those people out there could hear me playing, people I knew, like Mitch and Belle and Liesl and Gareth, people like Aunt Bridget, and I was happy I was playing for them, as well as for all the people I didn't know. Maybe there was a kid out there who was in a bad mood or something because he'd gotten into a fight with his mother or his brother and now maybe he'd walk into the park and forget what he was mad about.

Well, I *kind* of thought those thoughts. They flickered through my mind in a less clear way than I am writing about them. Mostly I was trying to concentrate on not messing up.

I finished, and Mr. P. was playing alone, the last four notes, when he exploded into a cough. He lunged for the Off switch. "Damn!" he said. It took him a minute to regain his breath. He hung the violin back up on the wall and then took mine and hung it up, too.

"That was fun," he said finally.

"Yeah," I said. I felt exhilarated. Maybe playing the music was even better than hearing the music! He opened a desk that was tucked into a corner of the room—it was all gleamy wood, too—and brought out a piece of sheet music. "Think you can learn this?" he asked. He played it for me; it was a nice tune and wasn't too complicated. I thought I'd be able to learn it in time, with him, following him, but he said, "Take the music back to your aunt Bridget's and learn it."

Now for the awful truth. "I can't read music," I said. I thought of the times I'd tried. Music on a page always seemed to panic me. The black notes made me dizzy and slightly sick to my stomach; they were a secret code I couldn't figure out.

"You play the way you do and you can't read music?" I thought the wrinkles in Mr. P.'s forehead were going to shoot right off the top of his head. "That's incredible!" I cringed slightly, waiting for the scolding. He paced a bit, shaking his head. "What a good ear you must have, Willy. Well, just think what you'll be able to do when you *can* read music!"

I stared at him. He wasn't scolding me—in a way he was praising me. And he was taking it for granted I *would* learn. He wasn't moaning and groaning like my father would have been, or calling me lazy. He wasn't being worried like my mother, who sometimes acted as if I were so pathetic I was beyond help.

He took a pencil out of his desk. "I'll write the names of the notes in for you and pretty soon you'll memorize them." He frowned a little and shook his head. "You shouldn't, you know, get too formal about lessons or anything until you're older. There's something original and sincere about your playing that shouldn't get ruined. All right?"

I nodded, not knowing what my mother would have to say about that. All I knew was that I was going to learn how to read music even if it did make me feel crazy and sick to my stomach. I'd just have to get over it.

Somewhere in the apartment a clock chimed two

o'clock. With a little stab of remembering, I thought of Gareth and baseball practice. "I have to go now," I said to Mr. P. "I promised Gareth Pugh—he's our manager—I'd practice today. He's really happy the park is saved. We have a baseball team and his dream is to beat this other team called the Sharks." I had a thought. "You wouldn't want to come watch us, would you?"

"Why . . . yes, I would," he said. "Nothing would please me more."

"But who'll play the music?"

"Oh, the people can learn to live without it, here and there. Little silences in the web of their lives."

"You'll have to start signing other people up so you can take breaks."

"Yes, I guess I will. Think they'll like playing here?"

"Are you kidding? Of course they will!" I grinned at him and he laughed and then he coughed and I sighed. Even as he coughed, he pulled out a ciga-rette.

twenty-three

Even though I had
to leave my home,
I'm happy now on this island.
It's beautiful, and I love this place.

—*Arethusa*

Mr. P. sat and watched our practice. I missed hearing the music in the background while I was planted out there by first base, but the next best thing was to have him watching us. It was a totally different experience from having my parents on the sidelines. For one thing, Mr. P. laughed a lot. Every time someone missed a pitch or fumbled the ball, we'd hear his smoky laugh. But mostly we played well—better than usual, I'd say. I guess we were all happy to know the park was safe, and even Gareth was dishing out the praise. "Way to go, Toenail!" he'd shout. "Hey, you're hot today, Hoscowitz."

Afterward I introduced Mr. P. to everyone. The kids gathered around and I felt proud, almost as if I had invented him or something. He congratulated Gareth on running a fine team. "Who's the team to beat?" he asked.

"The Sharks," said Gareth. "They're good, and they're tough."

"Well, you ought to be able to knock the stuffing out of them."

"I don't know," Gareth said seriously. "They've been playing longer than we have, and they're older and bigger."

"Not smarter, though," Mr. P. said seriously.

Gareth nodded, too oblivious to notice that Mr. P. was having fun with him. "Mostly they're not. Their pitcher, though, Dillon Deronda, he's pretty savvy. Pretends he isn't. That's the most dangerous kind. I guess that's why they call themselves the Sharks— they sneak up on you and tear you apart."

"Your team have a name?" Mr. P. asked. He took out a handkerchief and wiped the sweat off his head. He wasn't used to being out in the sun, I thought.

"He can't decide," Dixon said. "He changes it every day. We've been the Gill Park Gila Monsters, the Gill Park Gang, the Gill Park Greasers, the Gill Park Grasshoppers."

"*Grasshoppers?*" Mr. P.'s eyes widened. The other kids smirked, but Gareth continued to look serious.

"I wanted something that was different from the Sharks—more subtle, you know."

"Hmmm," said Mr. P., wiping his forehead again.

"But it doesn't quite do it for me," said Gareth.

"No," Mr. P. agreed.

"Hey, Mr. Pettingill, get back to playing your music," Toenail said, stepping forward. "I like that Mozart sonata, the one you play on Sunday mornings."

"You noticed?" Mr. P. asked faintly.

Toenail scowled at him. "Why wouldn't I?" he asked. "You've always played it. I thought you dropped dead or something when the music stopped. It was totally weird without it. And I like that Respighi, the one you play when it's stormy."

Mr. P. shook his head and threw up his arms. "And I was thinking no one noticed or cared."

"That's cuz you're always up there, dude," said Toenail. He nodded his blue head in the direction of Mr. P.'s apartment. "Can't know that much if you're always up there."

"I know I'm delighted to meet *you*," said Mr. P., getting up. He put out a hand. "Your name is . . . ?"

"Toenail," said Toenail in a gruff voice.

"Toenail," Mr. P. repeated, shaking his hand.

"Hey, dude, I'm out of here," said Hoscowitz. "Going swimming. I'm frying out here. Thanks, Mr. P., for the park and everything."

"Hey, man, thanks," the others said.

"It's astonishing," Mr. P. said when Liesl and Gareth and I were the only ones left. He stood up from the bench. "Who could have imagined a toenail of a kid with blue hair would care about Respighi's *Pines of Rome?*"

"But if he heard it all his life, why wouldn't he?" I said.

"Yes, I see your point," said Mr. P., nodding. He put a hand on my shoulder and wiped his face again. "It is beastly hot, though, in this park of mine. I should have thought to bring a hat."

"Here," said Gareth. He whipped off his baseball cap. Mr. P. took it gratefully.

"You are a generous young man," he said, putting it on. Gareth's hair was matted, slick with sweat, and I didn't like thinking about how that sweat might be feeling on Mr. P.'s bald head.

"Hey, it's nothing," said Gareth, his top lip sticking on his braces as he tried to smile. He licked it unstuck. "It's the least I can do. If it weren't for you, I'd just be a regular kid. Normal, boring." He grinned and his lip stuck again. "I gotta get going now, though. My dad got me these videos of famous baseball plays and I was trying to watch them last night, but I couldn't concentrate because of being worried and everything, so I'm gonna check them out now."

"I'll give your cap back to Willy," said Mr. P.

"No problem," said Gareth as he ran off.

"That boy has a future," said Mr. P., yanking at the visor of the cap. It was a little small and it looked funny on him.

"Yeah, a future in the bin for loonies," said Liesl. She was sitting on a bench, her baseball glove and chalk apron in her lap.

"In the bin for loonies," repeated Mr. P. "Where in the world would you have learned an expression like that?"

"Belle Vera," Liesl said. "She said that's where *you* belong." She grinned like a maniac, very pleased with herself.

"Oof," said Mr. P. "Thank you for sharing that with me. I suppose she is very angry with me. I must find her soon and apologize, although I was trying to do right by you." He sighed and looked at Liesl. "What was the best thing about your childhood?" he asked her.

Liesl cocked her head at him like a little bird. Her sharp, pointed face looked thoughtful. Then she spread out her skinny arms. "This," she said. "The park."

Mr. P. didn't say anything at first—he just stared at her, and then put back his shoulders and stood up straighter. "I'm glad" was all he finally said. "Well, then, Willy, where shall I go now? You must be my guide."

"You could just sit in your park for a while," I said, worried about him walking in the heat. "Get to know it, you know, just by being in it. You could sit on a bench by the fountain. It's pretty much in the middle."

"Well, yes it is, it's the heart of the park, by design. And when we're there, I'll tell you a story about it."

"And I can draw," said Liesl, leaping up. "I haven't drawn in the park since those stupid Do-littles."

As soon as we reached the fountain, Liesl dropped to the pavement and plunged her hand into her apron pocket. She drew a line with a piece of yellow chalk.

"Yeah," she said. "That's the stuff."

Mr. P. and I sat on one of the benches facing the fountain. Mr. P. took out a cigarette, lit it, and sat smoking, saying nothing for a moment. Then he said, "Once upon a time. . ."

I turned to look at him. "This is the story about the fountain?"

He nodded, pulling on the visor of Gareth's cap. "It comes from mythology, from the great poem called *The Metamorphoses* by a Roman named Ovid. The word *Metamorphoses* also means 'transformations.' So it goes like this: There was a young huntress named Arethusa. She lived in the forest, wild and free. Perhaps she led the life I imagined for this one," he said, nodding toward Liesl. "But anyway, one hot day, a day as hot as this one, Arethusa went out hunting and she became incredibly hot and sweaty. Well, she came upon this cool, clear brook. It was so clear that she could look down and see all the little stones in it."

"So she jumped in," said Liesl, head down as her fingers moved busily across the pavement.

Mr. P. snapped his fingers. "Precisely," he said. "Young Arethusa dived right in, but in that instant, she heard this gurgly voice calling to her from underwater."

"That's creepy," said Liesl. She stopped drawing for a moment and sat up to look at him.

"Well, it *was* creepy," Mr. P. agreed. "Arethusa was terrified. She sprang to the bank, and as she did so, the voice called out her name, *'Arethusa, Arethusa!'*"

"How'd whoever it was know her name?" Liesl asked.

"Well, it was Alpheus, the god of the brook, and gods know things. The important thing is he had fallen in love with her."

"Gross," said Liesl, hunching back over her drawing. "I would have been out of there."

"Well," said Mr. P., "she fled as fast as she could, but Alpheus left the brook and raced after her."

"Did he catch her?" Liesl asked, looking up again.

"Liesl!" I jumped up from the bench. "Let him tell the story, will ya?"

"I just wanted to know," Liesl whined.

"Well, he's going to tell you."

"Hush, both of you," Mr. P. said sternly. I sat back down, cramming my fists into my pockets. Liesl was *not* going to survive in a classroom. She'd *never* be able to keep her mouth shut. "Arethusa ran hard. She ran and ran, through the forest, up hill and down dale, as fast as she could. Alpheus wasn't faster, but he had, as they say nowadays, more endurance. She never looked behind her, but she could hear his footsteps and his breathing, and she could even feel his hot breath on the back of her neck."

"Huh!" said Liesl, unable to be quiet a minute longer. Her eyes were very bright and the blue vein blazed. "That's how I felt when I was on the bike and then I saw this cop behind me and then he started chasing me."

"How awful for you," Mr. P. said sympathetically.

"Well, go on," said Liesl.

Mr. P. lit a cigarette and then went on. "Alpheus was just about to get her when Arethusa called to her own special goddess to save her."

"Are-thu-mahingie, Alphie-oso," Liesl burst out. "What *are* these names?"

"If you're going to be a scholar, you'd better get used to names like this," said Mr. P. "And you'd better be quiet."

Liesl sat up very straight and stuck her nose in the air. "Yes, a scholar," she said proudly. "That's what I am. All right, I'll be quiet from now on. Go on."

Mr. P. took out his handkerchief and wiped his face. Even with the hat, he was sweating like crazy sitting there in the sun. Maybe hanging out in the park like this wasn't such a good idea. "Well, her goddess heard her, and the next thing Arethusa knew, the long locks of her hair, her fingers, her fingertips, her legs, her feet were all flowing like a stream."

Liesl was up off the pavement. She leaped around in front of us. "She was turned into *water*? *Cool!*"

"A stream," said Mr. P., smiling. "The goddess opened the earth, and Arethusa flowed into it, underground. She traveled underground for a long time, and finally came up a long way away, on an island, as a fountain."

We all stared at the fountain. Liesl ran over to it and stroked a hand through the spray. "Arethusa," she said.

"That's right," said Mr. P.

"Arethusa," said Liesl again. "I'm going to change my name to Arethusa."

Mr. P. put out his cigarette under the heel of his shoe and then picked up the butt and put it into his pocket. "I like thinking my fountain is Arethusa," he said. "And according to the story, she grew to love her new home."

Liesl sat on the edge of the fountain, playing with the water, and we watched people going by. I thought, in a way, that maybe by coming to the park, I'd taken a dive, too, and had come up in new place, in a different form.

"Hey, Mr. P., how'd you remember all that mythology stuff?" Liesl asked.

"I learned it when I was young, when I had time, when I stopped going to school," said Mr. P.

"I don't want to hear about how you think school is dumb." Liesl stood in front of him, hands on hips, ready for a fight.

"Let's count and see how many people go by in five minutes," I jumped in quickly. She hadn't had a tantrum in a while, and I could see she was on the edge.

"Okay. Get ready, set, go," said Mr. P. eagerly, only too happy to distract Liesl. He looked at his watch.

I counted kids with their parents—little guys who were hanging on to their mothers' hands, and big ones who were taller than their mothers. I counted women in sunglasses and men squinting against the sun. I counted women in sandals, men in white socks and black shoes, girls in red high-tops, girls in ankle bracelets, girls with pink toenails, guys in red high-tops, guys in black skateboard-type sneakers. I counted people with water bottles and people with fruit smoothies. I counted old men who walked pigeon-toed, teenaged guys who walked like macho men, and middle-aged men in suits who walked like middle-aged men in suits. I counted people who walked brisk walks, people who walked slow, heavy walks. I counted women with blouses tucked in with belts, and women with long shirts out. I counted serious-looking men with pens in their pockets; happy, chatty ladies carrying cloth bags with lots of stuff in them; old ladies carrying purses clutched against them; and young well-dressed men and women carrying briefcases. I counted girls in shorts and sleeveless blouses and tank tops and tons of guys in T-shirts. I counted a bunch more people with blue hair or almost white bleached blond hair and studded dog collars around their necks and a bunch with bandannas and a bunch with earrings, some in their ears, some on their eyebrows, some in their noses, some in their bellies.

"Done," said Mr. P.

"One hundred people just walked by us in five minutes," I said. "That's one hundred people who would have missed the park if it was a mall."

Mr. P. raised his eyebrows. "All one hundred of them?" he asked.

"Yep, every one of them," I said.

"Even these characters?" he asked.

I looked in the direction he was looking. I had been too busy counting to notice them before. Three boys who looked a little older than I was were lined up against the edge of the fountain, in a row, all without shirts on, two of them smoking cigarettes, and they had a huge boom box that they put down on the ground in front of them. They turned it on loud. The music had a heavy beat that banged into the air, into my ears, and I could feel it vibrating in the wood of the park bench and even underneath my feet.

I looked at the boys. They didn't care if we were there or not. They didn't care if we liked the music or not. Their faces had that kind of masky look kids get when they're pretending not to notice anything.

I thought of my feeble Pachelbel's Canon. I was embarrassed for myself. What was I thinking? That kids like this would be turned on by my one-note-at-a-time violin screeching?

I turned to Mr. P. "I don't know," I said at last. "Maybe not."

"Jumpin' Jiminy," said Liesl, sitting up and pushing back her cap. "Will ya look at what the cat dragged in! It's Dillon Deronda."

twenty-four

When I play the harmonica,
I can feel the notes come into my lungs.
I can feel the pressure of the notes,
and I like the big sound you get
out of something so small.
It makes me feel crisp.

—*Zack Mack*

The kid Liesl was pointing to was tall and had a kind of ratty-looking face, and even though he was wearing a baseball cap, you could see his hair was long and in a ponytail. So that was Dillon Deronda, the feared pitcher of the Sharks. "Hey, Mike," he said. "Where's the marker?"

"That's Spiky Mike," Liesl said out of one corner of her mouth. "He's a Shark, too, and so's the other kid with all the curly hair—he's Zack Mack."

The one called Spiky Mike was short and kind of stocky, and his hair was short and spiky. He pulled a big fat black marker out of his pocket. Mr. P., sitting beside me, tensed up. I guess we both had the same picture in our heads—of that marker being scribbled all over the fountain, right in front of us in full daylight, right in front of the owner of the park. Before I could even breathe another breath, Liesl had flung herself against him. "Gimme that, you ape!" she was screaming.

"What the—" Dillon reached a long arm over and in the next moment he and Liesl were in a tug-of-war over the marker. Dillon was taller and meaner than Liesl. He gave her a good dig with his elbow and then held the marker over her head. "Do you mind?" he asked, glaring at her.

Taking a big piece of cardboard out from under his other arm, he began writing on it with the marker. Then he sat down, all hunched up, in front of the fountain with the piece of cardboard propped up against his knees. He swiped the hat off his head and held it in front of him. Mr. P. collapsed back down on the bench and burst out laughing, then pointed at the sign. It said, SPARE CHANGE FOR A HUNGRY HUNGRY VEGAN.

Liesl was still fuming. "Turn off your stupid music," she said, sticking her face right in Dillon's face. She had a lot of nerve. I didn't know if I admired her or if I thought she was really dumb.

"It's a free country," he said, basically ignoring her. The other two boys snickered.

"It's stupid music," she said.

"Your opinion," he said. "And the big guy isn't playing right now."

"The big guy?"

"Mr. God Pettingill. Hey, I can put anything I want to into the airwaves."

"It just so happens that Mr. God Pettingill—"

But Mr. P. actually picked up a little stone from the gravel underneath the bench and threw it at Liesl. It popped her right in the shoulder.

"Hey!" she screeched. "What—" Then she saw Mr. P. shaking his head at her and putting his finger against his mouth, warning her not to say anything more.

"You're the noisiest person here," said Spiky Mike. "Why don't you, like, do a magic act, and disappear?"

"Funny, funny," Liesl said. "Why don't you?"

I went over to Liesl and pulled her away. She was like a scrappy little dog, always looking for trouble.

"Draw them," I muttered in her ear.

Her face lit up. "Yeah, I will," she said. She settled herself back down on the pavement. Relieved, I sat back down with Mr. P. At least now she wouldn't get beat up. Dillon pulled a bag of sunflower seeds out of his pocket and started stuffing them into his mouth. As the boom box boomed away, Dillon kept stuffing his mouth until it was bulgy and bumpy and filled up. Then he began spitting out the husks.

"Wow," said Mr. P. slowly. "A human rodent."

"Do you want to leave?" I asked him. He was looking hot and tired.

"Oh no," said Mr. P. "This is real life. I wouldn't miss it for anything."

I couldn't help thinking how my dad would have reacted to Dillon. He would have been fuming. "That boy should get a job instead of acting like a bum!" he would have said. And here Mr. P. was laughing at him.

"He's not hurting anyone," Mr. P. said, turning to me, as if reading my thoughts. He had to raise his scratchy voice in order to be heard over the music. "It's not a bad thing to think being a bum is romantic. By the time he's my age, he'll stop being idealistic and invest in the stock market and have a wife and three children and eat steak and potatoes every night for dinner—although he'll have to change some of his habits if he's going to get anyone to marry him," he added when Dillon spit again.

We watched the boys for a while. It was like watching a play. People who seemed to know them came by and stopped to talk for a minute. Some people threw money into Dillon's hat. He didn't even look at them or nod or say thank you or anything. It was weird how he acted as if no one existed but himself.

After a while Zack put out his cigarette, leaned down, and turned off the boom box. Then he stood up and took a harmonica out of his pocket and started playing. It was really jazzy. Spiky Mike started banging on the side of the boom box like it was a drum. You couldn't help feeling happy and moving your feet. Mr. P. sat nodding, tapping his feet, too. It changed the whole mood of this play we were watching, and also how I felt about these guys; well, Zack and Mike anyway, because Dillon Rat-Face was still crouched behind his sign, his face a total blank, just spitting away. A pretty big crowd gathered. Everyone cheered and clapped when Zack finished, and he passed Dillon's hat and a lot of coins got tossed into it. Then Dillon turned the boom box back on.

"He's darn good," said Mr. P.

"You should ask him to play for the park," I said.

"Think so?" Mr. P. asked.

"Yes," I said. "Think about it. How everyone'll bounce when they walk. Smile and stuff."

"He'll play at five o'clock and tired mothers won't yell at their children at the end of the day," said Mr. P., smiling as he thought about it. "The young will stand in the buses during rush hour and let the elderly sit down. Willy, my man, you have a good idea there."

He got up from the bench and walked over to Zack, who was sitting back down on the edge of the fountain, lighting another cigarette. Mr. P. stuck out his hand. "Hi," he said. "I'm Mr. God."

Zack looked startled. Spiky Mike looked startled. Even Dillon's eyebrows went up a little and he sort of turned his face—not too much, of course, because it wouldn't have looked cool to show much interest.

"I'd like you to play your harmonica for the park,"

Mr. P. said. "Five o'clock on weekdays. During rush hour. Thirteen East Park. I'll pay you. Pettingill is the name."

"Mr. Pettingill?" It was like a mask dropped off Zack's face and he smiled a really good smile. He turned off the music. "Hey, man, you *are* Mr. God. I saw your picture in the paper. You really want me to play?"

"You bet," said Mr. P. "What did you say your name was?"

"Zack Mack. Zachary S. Mack."

"Well, Zachary S. Mack, I'll be expecting you."

Zack ran a hand through his curly hair. "What about Mike here?" he asked, putting a hand on his friend's shoulder. "He plays a mean bongo drum."

Mr. P. looked thoughtful. "We'll see," he said. "We'll have an audition. He can come with you, but I'm not promising anything."

Spiky Mike grinned. "You'll like it," he said.

"What about your other friend?" Mr. P. asked, looking at Dillon. Dillon narrowed his eyes, just slightly, but otherwise it was as if he hadn't heard anything. What was with this guy? Was he on drugs or something?

Zack shrugged. "The only thing Dillon here is into is baseball," he said. "He started smoking when he was nine, but five days ago he decided to quit, cold turkey, because he said it was wrecking his game."

Mr. P. nodded. "So that explains the seed habit."

"And he doesn't eat meat," said Zack, proud of his buddy. "Or any animal products. So he can get healthy. So he can be the best baseball player in the world."

It was hard to believe this guy sitting all scrunched up on the pavement spitting seeds was the Dillon Deronda that Gareth was always talking about. He didn't look as if he had the energy to stand, much less throw a fastball. Liesl scrambled up from the pavement and peered into his face. "Hey, you, Mr. Talkative, I know a baseball team that's gonna beat your butt."

"Oooh, big talk," said Dillon, spitting.

Spiky Mike laughed. "Listen, you little pathetic excuse for a third baseman, you guys don't have a prayer."

"The Sharks are the best team in the park, *your* park, Mr. God," said Zack, sort of saluting Mr. P. as he said it. "Hey, good thing you didn't turn this place into a mall."

"See you at five o'clock," Mr. P. said. Then, turning to me, he said, "It's time, Willy, for me to head back home. I feel like a fried egg."

"And you look like one, too."

We all heard it, coming out of Dillon's mouth, a sort of mumble, but clear enough. But when we turned and looked at him, his face was completely expressionless, as if he had said nothing at all.

"Pleasant chap," said Mr. P. as we walked away.

But he quit smoking, I thought, but I didn't have the nerve to say it out loud to Mr. P. Besides, I didn't want to stick up for Dillon; he was such a creep. He didn't smoke anymore and didn't eat meat or hurt animals, but he was still a rat-faced shark.

"We're gonna wipe the grass with those Sharks," Liesl said in a tough little voice.

I sighed. "I don't know," I said. I looked back over my shoulder at the three boys. Zack Mack and Spiky Mike seemed normal enough, but they were older and bigger, and who knew what the rest of the team was like. Worst of all, their leader was Dillon Deronda. A shark was bad enough, but a rat-faced shark . . . I wasn't looking forward to standing there with a bat in my hand waiting for him to pitch a ball at me.

But Dillon sure was confusing because I had this idea that vegans ought to be gentle, nice people because they didn't want to hurt animals. Dillon didn't seem gentle or nice to me. I also felt as if I ought to admire him for quitting smoking, but how could I admire a guy who seemed like such a creep?

I was still thinking about Dillon when I realized we were walking right by Mitch's flower stand. Mitch was there, and Belle Vera too. What a meeting this was going to be. I held my breath as Belle approached.

"Madame," said Mr. P., bowing to her.

"Monsieur," she said, a little cool.

"You will forgive me, Madame?" asked Mr. P.

"What is it that you were taking into your head?" she asked, a little huffy. She crossed her arms over her chest. "What I mean to say is, what is it you were thinking about?"

"There have been times, in my life, Madame, when I have thought entirely too much," said Mr. P. "And my thoughts have guided me instead of reasonable common sense, but in the end, I did think the child needed a family."

"Perhaps, Monsieur, you repent too late." Belle Vera plumped her hands across her chest.

Mr. P. bowed his head. He did not seem to know what else to say.

A pair of fat birds approached, hopping along pretty boldly in front of Belle, as if they knew her. She pointed to them. "And how do you think these little doves of the park felt when the music was absent? So sad, so silent." She tossed them some whole-wheat crumbs from a bag she kept tied to her side. The birds acted very cool, bobbing their heads but not rushing to get the food.

"Don't be too hard on Mr. Pettingill," Mitch said, jumping in, hinting that Belle Vera had said enough. "Look at these birds. The birds of this park are very polite. This one says, 'You first,' and that one says, "No, no, you first.' It's a tribute to you, sir."

Mr. P. turned toward Mitch, looking like a little kid who's glad he's been rescued. "And you, Mitch Bloom—from what I hear, I am very much in your debt. And to think, you would have lost your home. I—I don't know what to say."

"Well, then, I say that in spite of a bit of heavy weather, the plant's still blooming, and I'd better take you up to my home and give you a bit of my best strawberry drink. I've a stunning crop of them this summer. You look all wilted, if I do say so myself. Belle, will you join us?"

There was a heavy pause as Belle seemed to consider. Then she shrugged. "I shall try to guard the silence and let the bygones be gone," she said.

"Thank you, Belle," said Mr. P. "And you will be a magnificent teacher for the child."

"I shall rejoice to teach the child," said Belle.

And so Mr. P., Belle Vera, Liesl, and I followed Mitch through the path in the woods. When we came to the base of the tree, Mr. P. looked up and shook his head. "A mighty oak," he said.

"I chose an oak to build my house in because oaks hang on to most of their leaves, even though they turn brown, through most of the winter, and I admire that in a tree," said Mitch.

"On tray, silver plate," said Liesl as she opened the elevator door.

"And to think," Mr. P. said as he stepped in, "I might have never experienced riding in this elevator if Willy hadn't gone looking for me."

Once up in the house, we sat in the living room while Mitch made refreshments. Mr. P. kept shaking his head, amazed by everything, and then it wasn't long before he and Mitch and Belle were discussing how to enlarge it.

All of a sudden, Liesl went right up to Mr. P. and stood in front of him. "I always wanted to ask you, were you ever married?" She had been scarfing down strawberries and she looked like she had blood all over her face and hands.

"The doves have more gentility than you have," Belle said disapprovingly. "The young do not demand such things from the old."

"It's all right," said Mr. P., laughing his choky laugh. "Everyone wonders about me, but they are either too polite or too afraid of me to ask." He coughed a long cough, and everyone looked embarrassed while we waited for him to stop. I felt a surge of anger. I wanted to pull the pack of cigarettes out of his pocket and shred them to pieces. "Ah, there," he said at last. "What was I saying? Oh yes, marriage. I didn't believe in marriage, just as I didn't believe in schools, but there was a wonderful woman. Her name was Tillie Willauer. She was an opera singer. Oh, how she could sing! Her voice soared to the heavens. I remember the first time I heard her sing. She was singing an aria from Mozart's *The Marriage of Figaro*." He was quiet for a minute, his wrinkles all soft from remembering. "She had webbed toes," he added.

Liesl giggled. "Webbed toes?"

"She was a remarkably beautiful woman who happened to have webbed toes. They say it is a sign of genius."

"What happened to her?" I asked.

"She wanted to get married," Mr. P. said. "So she married someone else. She had two kids and kept singing and has made a good name for herself And I—I have no children, no one to whom I can pass on my park, the work of my lifetime. I suppose that was another reason I thought I could abandon it." He shook his head. "Sometimes I do regret the choices I have made, but today I do not, for I have a park full of wonderful people."

Liesl started passing around the strawberry drinks from a tray, and I thought of my mother, who liked me to pass around nuts and things at her parties, and then I smiled, thinking how different this party was from my mother's parties. For one thing, she didn't have them in a tree house.

twenty-five

If you can win at baseball,

you can win at life.

—*Dillon Deronda*

It was the day of the game; there they all were, those Sharks, and they had uniforms—green pants and white tops with *Sharks* written on the back and a picture of a toothy shark's head on the front.

We huddled in a group, shocked, watching them as they warmed up. "Geez," Toenail muttered. "This isn't Little League. Where'd they get the moolah to get duded up like that?"

"Mike Zantos," Dixon said, jerking his head toward Spiky Mike. "He goes to my school. His family's loaded. They give him anything he wants."

We hadn't expected them to look so professional. And big. They were big and tough-looking, and Dillon Deronda, Mr. Robot out there on the pitcher's mound, his mouth full of sunflower seeds, spitting away, was the toughest of all.

"Come on, guys," Gareth said as we huddled together for the manager's pep talk. "It's intimidation, pure and simple. Don't let 'em psych you out. You guys are good, and don't you forget it."

But I think we did forget it. The Sharks were up first, and it was like they were wired, they had electricity inside them. They made two runs in about two seconds. Talk about demoralizing.

The hard part for me was that Mr. P. wanted, more than anything, to watch us. He didn't make me feel self-conscious the way my parents did, because I knew by now he just liked watching, and he didn't care that much if we won or not, but it meant there wasn't any music. I stood beside the bag, heart hammering in my throat, as Spiky Mike stepped up to the plate. All I could hear in my ears was my own pulse. I tried humming to myself. Dah dah dattee dah dah dah dah dah de duh dattee dah duh duh. The Trumpet Voluntary. Yeah, well, it was ridiculous and I knew it.

Mike wasn't a tall guy, but he was solid, and he swung that bat like he had been born with it. *Ping,* the bat made contact and the ball went whistling past my right ear. So now it was three runs in the first half of the first inning. Not a good way to begin. Not a good way to go on. We couldn't seem to rally. It was like our reflexes were dead. Death by slow torture. The Sharks weren't even breaking a sweat.

At the bottom of the fifth, score six to zip, we huddled together. Gareth's freckles stood out against his pale face. "What's the deal, guys?"

Capasso shook his head. "I don't know. They beat us from the start. We just aren't ready yet."

"We're not playing like a team," said Hoscowitz. "It's like we're all separate molecules, like we're not communicating."

I nodded. That's just what it felt like. I glanced over at Mr. P. His wrinkles were saggy and he looked concerned. I thought I knew what was missing. I went over to him. "Do you think you could go and play us some music?" I asked. "Something upbeat. I think it would help. I know you have to walk all the way back and everything."

He plunked a hand on my shoulder. "If I can get you boys out of the hole," he said, "I'd walk ten miles and play two hundred symphonies. But I think you guys need a name. And uniforms. I'll even buy 'em if you come up with an idea."

It took him a while to get back to his apartment, a whole inning, but we were beginning to wake up. They didn't score on us, and we at least finally got our bases loaded, even if Toenail did pop a fly to right field and Zack Mack scooped it right out of the air, no problem.

By the top of the sixth, the airwaves were dancing, and I mean dancing. Mr. P. was playing a waltz on the violin—its corny three-four time made me laugh out loud. Only Mr. P. would think of playing a waltz for a baseball game. It was as if he were saying, "Look, this is your first try, and it's okay. Don't take it all so seriously."

I loosened up then. When one of the Sharks smacked one right to first, I didn't even flinch while I stuck out my glove and caught it smooth as ice cream. I whaled that ball to Hoscowitz and he whaled it right over to second, where a kid had been leading off for third. Reflexes all working perfectly. Hey, we were a team—we'd just figured it out a little too late.

The score was six-four by the end. Zack Mack and Spiky Mike and their buddies were whooping it up; Dillon Rat-Face stood quietly, not moving a muscle, but his whole body, ponytail and all, did the talking: he was feeling superior, all right.

"Okay, guys, not perfect, but respectable," said Gareth. I thought he'd be madder than spit, but he was a pro, right down to every freckle; he made us line up and shake hands. Liesl didn't want to, but Gareth pushed her into line. "Rematch in three weeks," he said.

Rat-Face nodded. "We'll be there," he said.

"I hope you like your eggs scrambled fine," said Liesl.

"Ooh, big talk from a little girl, if you *are* a girl— are you sure you're human?" Dillon said.

"Knock it off," said Gareth.

We walked away from the field. The waltz music played, one two three, one two three. I leaped around on the field and threw my hat up in the air.

"What are you so happy about?" Gareth grumbled as he walked away.

I wasn't too sure I could tell Gareth I didn't care about losing. I'd just played the first baseball game of my life and I had survived it. More than survived—I hadn't even played that badly. Even my dad would have been proud of me—well, *maybe* he would have been—and then I thought, aw, who cares, *I'm* proud of me.

Just then Jerry Rabinowitz came up to us. He was beaming from ear to ear. "Listen to this, guys, this is my latest:

> *The green-eyed god of greed*
> *Planted a seed*
> *It was a weed*
> *Called money*

> *The green-grassed land I grieved*
> *It was my need*
> *To have it freed*
> *From money*

> *And it was, oh yeah, and it was, oh yeah,*
> *   and it was, yeah, yeah, yeah!"*

Jerry made the last line sound half gospel, half Beatles. As he walked away, Gareth and I looked at each other and burst out laughing.

"Maybe not his best poem," said Gareth.

"Yeah, but it sums everything up," I said. "It's why I can't be too bummed about losing. Because everything's all right." I looked around. "Oh yeah, oh yeah, oh yeah!" I leaped into the air again.

"I guess you're right," said Gareth when I had settled down. "If we hadn't almost lost the park, I would have been a lot more bummed than I am.

Nearly losing the park made me forget I had so much riding on this game." We walked by Sammy's hot dog stand. "Come on, I'll treat," he said. "Reward for playing good."

"Do you really think I played good?" I asked.

Gareth scowled at me. "I don't say things like that unless I mean them. Today you looked like uncooked spaghetti."

"Um, is that good or bad?"

"Cooked spaghetti, Willy, picture it. It's limp. It's all floppy."

"Oh."

"But today you were uncooked. You stood up straight."

"Oh."

"Not at first. But you got there."

He bought two hot dogs and we smeared them with "the works," ketchup, mustard, relish, and sat down on a bench to eat them.

"But we weren't ready," Gareth went on from where he had left off. "Plain and simple, we weren't ready. We haven't even played any other teams yet. It's like we jumped into this stone cold, and plus there's been so much stress lately because of Mr. P. selling and Liesl not being here and we didn't make the most out of our practices. I never should have put us up against them so early." He kicked the ground with his sneaker.

"But it wasn't that bad, Gareth. And we're gonna have a rematch."

Gareth bit into his hot dog and frowned. "I never was a good loser."

"I guess you're not used to it," I said.

"Yeah, everything else comes easy to me." Then his whole body seemed to straighten and he cheered up. "Let's go hit balls."

"Hit balls?"

"Yeah, my dad bought me a pitching machine. Let's go hit balls."

"Man, you're obsessed."

"Yeah, that's me."

So we spent the rest of the afternoon in Gareth's backyard and it actually felt good to be swinging away, hearing that *ping* when the contact was good, and everything stayed good for the next few weeks.

There are times when you forget about all the stuff that's happened in your life, and you forget to think about all the stuff that's going to happen in your life. You just wake up and ride with the day, and that's how it was for me, smack in the middle of the summer in Gill Park, smack in the middle of the city of Gloria.

Every morning I'd wake up, listening for the music. I was learning the names of the composers of pieces that I liked—Aunt Bridget would tell me, or Mr. Pettingill. They were Mozart and Bach and Beethoven, Handel and Gershwin, Debussy, Scott Joplin, Satie, Villa-Lobos, Brahms—and there were also jazz and ragtime and Beatles tunes and tunes from musicals. Mr. Pettingill played so much it was hard to keep track of it all. Well, every morning I'd listen for a while, and then jump out of bed, knowing that the day was going to be a good one. I'd go out to the kitchen to eat my cereal—if Liesl hadn't already eaten it all. Liesl was staying with us, helping Aunt Bridget with the gorillas, until Mitch could finish adding on to his house. After breakfast, Aunt Bridget and Liesl would work on the gorillas, and I'd practice the violin.

Later, Liesl and I would go to the park and she'd start drawing, with the music in the background. Liesl was drawing portraits on paper now and selling them. It was amazing to watch her; her long fingers knew exactly how to capture a person. She said she was earning money for Mitch. Mitch, meanwhile, was leading a "Clean Up the Park" campaign, and you'd see people painting benches and raking and planting more flowers.

I'd watch Liesl draw for a while, and then she'd go learn something from Belle Vera. You could tell how happy Belle was to be teaching again, and every time I saw her she was praising Liesl. "That child," she'd say, "she has the brains, and she is like the little *bouledogue,* all of the time she goes *grr grr,* so fierce, she desires so much to learn."

While Liesl was with Belle, I'd go to Mr. P.'s for a violin lesson, although because he so much didn't believe in lessons, he'd say we weren't having a lesson, we were just getting together for him to show me some things.

Well, whatever it was, I was learning, because one day I was looking at a piece of music when I felt a click inside my brain. I swear I could feel something actually slide over inside my head and the notes suddenly made sense to me. I started to piece together a tune of my own, writing, once I'd figured them out, the notes down on paper. I was pretty proud of my tune, and in my room, with Sophie on the bed, I'd play it over and over again. Liesl said I was driving her crazy, but Aunt Bridget said she liked hearing violin music in the apartment again, it just felt right, so I went right on working on it.

Sometimes Liesl and Gareth and I would meet in the park for lunch, with Mitch and Belle. Sometimes we'd go back to Aunt Bridget's. Sometimes we'd meet the guys before baseball practice. And sometimes I'd pinch myself. *I have friends,* I'd think.

In the afternoon, we'd have baseball practice or we'd play a pick-up game against other kids, usually an assortment of league and non-league kids. It wasn't anything formal, just fun, because it was all just kids who loved to play ball. It was where my playing got better because it didn't count; I could relax. And Gareth seemed to be having a good time, too, insulting us less, cheering us on more.

But as our match with the Sharks grew closer, Gareth began to yell again. He was really edgy, but we were too. Every once in a while we'd notice one of the Sharks watching us, Spiky Mike or Zack, but never Dillon. We figured he'd sent them out to spy on us. The weird thing was we never saw *them* practicing. We wondered when and where they did. Knowing Dillon, they probably got up in the dead of night. Maybe sharks aren't nocturnal, but rats are.

twenty-six

Any race, color, or creed can swim in my pool
as long as they don't use it as a bathroom.

—*Eda Nugget*

A lady named Mrs. Nugget had a swimming pool
over in the South Park, and all the parents let kids go
because there were lifeguards and also she let kids
swim for free. Gareth told me he didn't like to go
because so many bodies were usually broiling around
you could hardly see the water. But a couple of days
before our rematch with the Sharks, it was so hot,
Gareth's freckles were practically falling off his face.

"All right," he said to me after practice. "We're
gonna do it. We're going to Nugget's. But you have
to be careful. You have to watch out for people jumping on you. You could get your nose broken from
some kid kicking you in the face. And I have to intro-
duce you to Mrs. Nugget. She likes to know who all

the kids are, and she'll take you into her place and show you where the bathroom is."

We headed south across the park, Gareth on a slick ten-speed his dad had given him for his birthday, me on Uncle Roger's old three-speed. Lucky thing it was old, though, because when Liesl had been caught by the cop that day Roland Brookings had sent the entire police force of Gloria out looking for her, the bike had been left behind. Gareth and I had found it leaning against a tree; it reminded me of a trusty old mutt who wouldn't leave a spot if you told it to stay. I was glad for Uncle Roger's sake that it hadn't been stolen.

As we rode along, it occurred to me that each side of the park had its own personality. The North, where Aunt Bridget lived, was sort of run down, but it was artsy and interesting, with small theaters and junk shops and, best of all, blocks of streets that were neighborhoods. The West was business, with tall office buildings and fancy stores and fancy art galleries. The South was the poorest section, and the houses and apartments were all crowded together, but it basically felt a lot like the North, with neighborhoods, and there were cafés, like the Heliotrope. The East, well, that was the ritzy residential side of town, with fancy apartments facing the park, big trees along the pavement, and classy little restaurants. And, I, Willy Wilson, who used to feel as if I didn't belong to anything, the more I explored and got to know the park, the more I felt as if I belonged to all of it.

The minute Gareth introduced me to Mrs.

Nugget, she gave me a hug, which was like being hugged by a big black sweaty marshmallow. Gareth told me she only wore black, for her husband, who had died of cancer maybe fifteen years ago.

"YOU COME INTO MY PLACE, WILLY, AND I'LL SHOW YOU AROUND," she said to me after that hug. I found out she never spoke normally; she always yelled at the top of her lungs. I guess it was how she kept order in that crazy swimming pool. Even with lifeguards, it was unbelievably noisy with hundreds of kids in it, screaming and laughing and playing games. She led Gareth and me into her place, which was just behind the pool; it was all on one floor, a bunch of rooms strung together. Compared to the outside, it was dark, and I stubbed my toe on a statue; and then I realized the place was crammed with statues, and as my eyes got used to the light, I realized the statues were all religious, saints and Virgin Marys.

"I HAVEN'T SEEN YOU IN A DOG'S AGE, GARETH. HOW DO YOU LIKE MY HAIR?" she asked Gareth.

"It looks . . . different," said Gareth. "But good," he added quickly. "Real good."

Her hair was in tight little curls, but I had never met her before, so I didn't know what it had looked like before.

"I'VE GOT A FELLA," she boomed. "THE FIRST REAL FELLA AFTER FIFTEEN YEARS. YOU KNOW WHAT IT'S LIKE TO BE PAID ATTENTION TO BY A REAL MAN AFTER FIFTEEN YEARS? I'M TELLING YOU, THIS HAIRDRESSER IS A REAL

HUNK. THE LORD IS WATCHING OVER ME, HE REALLY IS."

We nodded politely, happy for her. You couldn't help liking Mrs. Nugget and wanting her to be happy. "I JUST WANTED YOU TO KNOW WHERE THE BATHROOM IS, WILLY," she said. "DON'T YOU GO USING MY POOL LIKE A BATHROOM LIKE SOME DIRTY KIDS I KNOW." She pointed to her bathroom. I thought it was pretty nice of her to let kids come into her house. As if she knew what I was thinking, she said, "I DON'T HAVE ANYTHING TO STEAL, SO I NEVER WORRY ABOUT KIDS COMING IN HERE. BUT EVEN IF THEY DID, I'D KNOW WHO DID IT, AND THEY'D FEEL SO GUILTY THEY WOULDN'T SLEEP AT NIGHT, AND THEY KNOW THEY'D FEEL THAT WAY, AFTER EVERYTHING I DO FOR THEM. THE GOOD LORD WATCHES OUT FOR ME AND I WATCH OUT FOR THEM. POOR LITTLE KIDDIES, SOME OF 'EM DON'T HAVE ANYONE TO LOOK OUT FOR THEM. SOME I GIVE BREAKFAST, SOME I MAKE SURE THEY GO TO SCHOOL, SOME I HELP OUT WHEN THEY GET IN TROUBLE." She looked at me long and hard. "YOU DON'T LOOK LIKE ONE OF THOSE TYPES, THOUGH, WILLY; YOU LOOK LIKE A REAL NICE KID. WHERE YOU FROM?"

I told her I was visiting my aunt Bridget McTaggart and, like everyone else, Mrs. Nugget knew who she was. She nodded and gave a big smile. "WELL, NOW, WILLY, YOU GET OUT THERE AND SWIM; AND GARETH, YOU LET ME KNOW IF ANY OF THOSE PUNKS GIVES YOU TROUBLE. SOME-

TIMES THEY SEE A NEW KID AND THEY ACT LIKE SHARKS."

Sharks was right. First I saw Zack Mack, flirting his head off in the middle of a bunch of girls, and then I saw Spiky Mike, throwing a beach ball to another kid I recognized as their third baseman. It seemed like everywhere I looked, there was a Shark, but no sign of Dillon Rat-Face.

The water felt good, even though there were all these kids in it. There was so much commotion—kids jumping, splashing, leaping up and shouting *Marco*, and other kids shouting back *Polo*. Then we found Toenail and Hoscowitz.

"Let's play eeling," said Gareth.

"Eeling?"

"You have to get from one end of the pool to the other without being touched once."

We had a blast, zipping around between legs. Every once in a while we'd hear Mrs. Nugget's voice booming over the kid noise. She'd yell something like, "HEY, YOU, ERIC, IN THE BAGGY YELLOW SHORTS, I CATCH YOU RUNNING AGAIN AND I'LL RUN YOU TO TIMBUKTU, YOU HEAR?" She'd be standing there in her black dress, shaking her fist, and the kid in the baggy yellow shorts would flash her a big grin. "I hear you, Mom," he'd call, and then leap into the pool and come up shaking his head like a wet dog, grinning from ear to ear. A lot of the kids called Mrs. Nugget Mom.

After playing eeling for a while, we all were standing by the edge of the pool, just taking a break, watching all the commotion, when all of a sudden, one by one, *bang bang bang bang,* one after the other, Gareth, Toenail, Hoscowitz, and I got shoved into the pool. I landed with a thwack against another kid. "Hey!" the kid yelled. "Whatcha think you're doing?" When I came up, I heard Mrs. Nugget's voice booming loud and clear. "HEY, YOU, DILLON DERONDA, I SAW THAT AND YOU GET OUT OF THE POOL RIGHT NOW."

I scanned the mass of heads in front of me, looking for Dillon, and there he was, slinking up from the water, miles away from us. He must have shoved us and then dived for the deep and swum away from us at a hundred miles an hour. He was a water rat, that's what he was, his long hair in the ponytail all slicked down wet.

"I WENT TO COURT FOR YOU AND DON'T YOU FORGET IT!" Mrs. Nugget yelled. "YOU BEHAVE IN MY SWIMMING POOL."

Dillon didn't call back, "Yes, Mom," or anything else for that matter. Ignoring Mrs. Nugget, he just sank under the water and disappeared.

The others were up on the side of the pool. I scrambled up and stood next to them. Gareth's whole body was quivering. "Dillon Deronda," he said, sputtering.

"What a jerk," said Toenail.

"Typical," said Hoscowitz.

"What'd he go to court for?" I asked.

The guys looked at each other and shrugged. "Dunno," said Toenail.

"Being alive," said Gareth, feeling the back of his neck. "That really hurt."

"Let's get him back," said Toenail. "Hold him under for a few minutes. See how he likes that."

"HEY, YOU, JANALYN, IN THE RED STRIPES, DON'T RUN I TOLD YOU THAT A MILLION TIMES!"

We watched as Mrs. Nugget barreled down on a little girl in a red-striped bathing suit. "OUT!" she was yelling. "OUT!"

"I won't do it again, I promise," the little girl whined.

"YOU BETCHA YOU WON'T," she boomed.

"I guess if we tried to drown Dillon, she'd notice," said Gareth.

"Let's go," said Toenail. "I don't want to be here if he's here."

"We can't let him affect us like that," said Gareth.

I knew Gareth's stubbornness. I could also see Dillon and a bunch of the other Sharks gathering at the other end of the pool. Even with all the other noise, I could hear loud guffaws coming from them, a sort of fake laughter. I knew that laughter. I heard it all the time from ninth-grade boys at school. It was a bonding laughter, like after they'd pushed some little kid in the trash can in the locker room. I didn't want to stay at all. I was about to drag Gareth out of there when there was a little gap in the yelling, the way there is sometimes when a bunch of people who are really noisy all seem to shut up at the same time. And into the gap came harmonica music and bongo drums.

It was like a bolt of lightning hit the pool and filled everyone with this jazzy, happy energy. I looked over at

Dillon's group. Zack wasn't there; Mike wasn't there. I figured it must be five o'clock and they were playing for Mr. Pettingill. Just knowing that made me not care about Dillon so much. I mean, if one of the enemy could be playing music in Mr. P.'s apartment, then it couldn't be such a bad enemy.

I dived into the pool. Gareth dived after me. Toenail and Hoscowitz followed. A beach ball was floating beside me as I came up. We played eel catch—you had to zap the ball with your fist as it came toward you. We stayed in the water the whole time Zack and Mike played, and then some more, until our eyes were soaked in chlorine. The next time I looked at Dillon, he was blurry and fuzzy.

twenty-seven

Don't forget, gorillas are
gentle, patient, and methodical,
while sharks are sensitive to the scent of blood
and circle their prey before attacking.
—*Bridget McTaggart*

I was sitting in the living room reading a letter my Mom had sent me.

"Dear Willy, things have been surprisingly busy while you've been gone. Sarah McMirtle asked me to be treasurer of the Parents' Association and the last person who held that post made quite a mess of things, so I'm having to start from scratch. Your father has been trying to hire a new assistant and has been enjoying the interviewing. He comes home rubbing his hands together saying, "Brains and ambition everywhere I look." He may be coming to Gloria on business and will stop by and see you. I do hope you are finding time to read and play the violin—I don't mean to be a little annoying bird on your shoulder, but you know you'll never get better unless you practice, and your violin teacher does say you have potential. Take care, Sweetie. Love, Mom.

I let the letter drop to the floor and looked out the window. We had one day left before our game; we were coming together as a team, but we were edgy, worried. Mom's letter only made me feel edgier, as if some yucky, sticky drink had been spilled all over me.

Aunt Bridget was out. She'd left a note on Flora. "Gone to face the cereals. XXOO B." I had to laugh. Aunt Bridget had decided she was going to give a dinner party, the first one since Uncle Roger had died, and invite Mr. P., Mitch Bloom, Belle Vera, Gareth (and Liesl and me, of course), so she had to go to a supermarket and get real food, as she put it. She wanted to stock up on cereal, too, but she spent quite a while complaining about supermarkets and all the choices they made you make, like with cereals in particular.

"Did you know, Willy," she had ranted, "that the last time I counted there were eighty-eight different kinds of cereals to choose from?"

"I don't care which kind," I had said, "as long as it's totally coated with sugar."

She came in the door at the same moment the phone rang. "Go down and bring up bags, will you please, Willy, while I answer the phone?"

When I came back up the stairs, Aunt Bridget was sitting at her worktable, shaking her head. "You're not going to believe what that phone call was about," she said.

My heart sank. "Mr. P. is selling the park after all."

"No, no, it's not that! It's something so silly, you're just not going to believe it." She put back her head and began laughing. When she stopped, she wiped her eyes and said, "All right, are you ready?" I nodded. She stood up from the table. She stood on a chair. "Announcing the very strange fact that the Palace just called and they don't *want* the gorilla costumes anymore!"

"Are you *serious*?"

"They're afraid the girls won't be able to dance in them. They want me to make pink flamingos instead."

I looked at her, wide-eyed. "But all that work—"

Aunt Bridget jumped off the chair. "It's okay—they're paying me. Handsomely. Where they get the money to throw around like that, I don't know, but who cares, that's what I say. Well, Willy, I guess we've graduated from black fuzz to pink feathers!"

She walked over to the rack of gorilla suits. "Do you know, Willy, I rather like these guys. I'm gonna miss them, but I guess I'll have to find a place to store them. There isn't really room in the apartment."

Mr. P.'s music came in the window. He was playing the piano today. Then I heard a whistling down in the street. I stuck out my head and saw Gareth and Liesl. "C'mon, Willy," Gareth called up. "It's time for practice."

And then I looked at Aunt Bridget and said, "Couldn't we use the gorillas as uniforms?"

Aunt Bridget looked back at me and grinned. "The Gill Park Gorillas," she said. "What a fabulous idea."

"You're brilliant," Gareth said when I told him. And that practice was the best practice we ever had. Now we couldn't wait to meet those Sharks, and I couldn't wait to see Dillon Deronda's face when he saw us. The big question was, would he actually move a muscle or would he just stay cool, really cool?

Well, we didn't have to wait long to find out. Our face-off was the next day. Most of the Sharks went into hysterics when we marched onto the playing field, ten (nine team members plus Gareth) gorillas beating our fists against our chests. Most of them even clapped. Not Rat-Face, though. He looked like he was going to spit sunflower seeds all over us.

Gareth got us into a huddle and gave us the pep talk of our lives.

"Now, listen up, guys. They're better than us, okay, and bigger, but we've got more heart. You gotta stay in the game and be aware of the base runners and the hitter. Know how many strikes there are and where everyone is. Got it, guys? Keep your head in the game, and whatever you do, Liesl, don't pout."

"Don't pout yourself," said Liesl. There was a tense moment as we waited for more—for her to kick Gareth or bite him or something—but that's all she said, and she said it with sort of a grin.

"You, Hoscowitz," Gareth went on, "don't forget to mix up the pitches, and stick with that split-fingered fastball—it has good movement. And for their big guys, keep it low. If you throw meat, we're all meat."

Hoscowitz nodded and blew a huge bubble with the gum he was chewing.

"When things get hot, and they're gonna get hot, keep up the chatter. Slap your gloves, wipe the sweat outta your eyes." He grinned and his braces gleamed in the sun.

"Scratch the fleas outta your fur and eat 'em," Toenail suggested.

"Roll in the dirt with your mate," said Capasso.

"Yeah," said Gareth, pleased. "That's the idea. Don't let 'em know we're nervous, and most of all, don't do a lot of thinking. You gotta have reflexes, guys, reflexes—all the stuff we've worked on this week. We're the Gill Park Gorillas, guys—so get out there and play ball!"

We'd put a sign up announcing THE GORILLAS MEET THE SHARKS, and our game had drawn quite a crowd. The Shark fans were on one side, the Gorilla fans on the other. Gareth's dad (and I'd finally gotten to meet him—he was a huge roly-poly guy who talked to

Gareth like they were the same age), Aunt Bridget, Mitch Bloom, and Belle Vera sat together on chairs that Mitch had brought. Mrs. Nugget, I noticed, was on the other side. Oh well, *someone* had to cheer for the other side. But then even Old Violet shuffled over to watch.

"Wonder who *she's* rooting for," I said to Gareth when I noticed her.

"She'll probably scream, 'Ha! You stink, *ha!*' at all of us!"

Well, it was time to start. The Sharks were first up to bat. Gareth had told me to play in front of the bag, and it gave me the jitters, but not as bad as I would have felt without the gorilla suit on. For the first half of the first inning we'd decided to keep the costumes on. We knew, after that, we'd fry in them, and that running bases might be a little difficult to manage, but it sure did feel like a good way to begin things. I stood there, rocking on my heels, ready to have them rip the ball my way, even though the butterflies were having a party in my stomach.

But then good old Mr. P. started in with the saxophone—he'd said he was going to play the sax for the game, a samba or a bossa nova. The air filled with these notes—these happy, dancing notes—and I felt like dancing myself. I felt as if I could do anything. The first three batters hit grounders to me, but I had the safest of hands, and I fielded them like a pro.

Then it was our turn to bat. We shed our gorilla skins, but still, were we slick! Even with Dillon Deronda whipping balls at him, Capasso hit a line drive to right center field that dribbled to the wall and those Sharks couldn't handle it. He ended up on second—right next to Mike with the spiky hair, but poor old Mike, he didn't look that perky. Then Hoscowitz drilled one to the left and it carried over the wall, driving in Capasso and himself. Two runs in the first ten minutes! I didn't get a chance to hit—we didn't bat around to me—but, looking at Dillon's face, his eyes narrowed, his jaw working on those seeds, I wasn't too disappointed. He called for a huddle, and I could see Zack pulling on his curly hair, the stress making him pull it straight up.

Next inning, the Sharks blasted in two home runs. Next inning, Liesl smashed one in for us. So, back and forth, back and forth, that's how things went the whole game, until it was the bottom of the ninth, and we were tied with one out and I was up. I'd been up two times, but I hadn't made contact with the ball yet. I knew I wouldn't—I just couldn't. Part of it was me, the old me, the me from back home who felt nervous about getting hit, that psyched myself out whenever the going got tough. Part of it was Dillon. He psyched me out. He was so expressionless I couldn't stand it.

I heard their catcher say, "Easy out" as I stepped up to the plate.

"Move in, move in, move in," Dillon drawled in a sort of bored voice to the fielders. "The little chump is up." And then I swear he ripped that ball right at my head. I couldn't help it. I flinched and stepped out too early and it broke right over the plate. *Stri-i-i-ke one!"*

"Smoke," the catcher said with a little laugh.

My hands were sweating so bad I could barely hold on to the bat. *Breathe,* I told myself. *You can do this.* I was about to step back up to the plate when Liesl appeared next to me. She was holding a gorilla mask. "Wear this," she said. "You're afraid of the ball. This'll protect your face."

"I'll look like an idiot," I said.

"Not any worse than you look now," she said.

I put on the mask and pressed my hand against it. Yeah, it felt hard. It would protect me. I stepped up to the plate. I heard that creep of a catcher snickering behind me. I wanted to step back and kick him in the face, but Dillon was winding up. That second pitch was another curveball, but I picked up the seams and judged the break perfectly. *Ping!* Well, it was a bloop to left field—easy to get—but the infielders didn't have time to react because they were so stunned when I actually hit the ball. Man, I ran so fast to first base I must have looked like a blur.

All the Gorillas were up, leaping up and down, beating on their chests. "Way to go, Wilson, way to go!"

"Vill-ee! Vill-ee! Go, Vill-ee!" I heard Belle Vera's voice rise above the others. I kept the mask on. I was a Gorilla now, for sure, and I was proud to wear that mask. And the saxophone was going like crazy. *Yes!* I raised my fist in the air.

Capasso, our best hitter, was up next. First pitch, he swung too early. Strike one. Second pitch was a fastball. He cracked a line drive down the right-field line. The right fielder, Zack, played it off the hop perfectly, but it was enough to bring me around to third. Runners on the corners, and Hoscowitz, our second best hitter, was up. Things were looking good. I snuck a glance at Dillon. His eyes were gleaming rattily. Yeah, I could sense a little stress in him. He wasn't such a cool customer. Then I glanced at Gareth and saw him give Capasso the steal sign.

Oh man, I was supposed to do something, but what was it? I remembered talking about this situation in practice. I tried to hold it in my mind: *Capasso's supposed to steal second, and if the catcher throws it down, I go home.*

God, if we keep this up, I, Willy Wilson, am gonna make it home. I'm gonna break the tie.

I was so antsy it was all I could do not to shoot right off the bag.

And then, out of the corner of my eye, I saw a tall man and a small woman. They were standing with Aunt Bridget. My heart sank. How long had *they* been here? What were *they* doing here?

Oh, Hoscowitz, rip it, rip it. . . . Come on, now, Hoscowitz. . . . Yeah, and what if he does and I run the wrong way, the way I always do when my dad is watching me, or what if I can't get my feet to move off third base?

First pitch. Capasso stole. Sure enough, the catcher threw it down. Sure enough, my legs seized up. *"Run, Willy, run home!"* I heard Gareth yelling, but home seemed too far away. Capasso slid into second. "Safe!" the ump called as the second baseman tagged him. I didn't look over at my dad, but I could feel him there. I could *feel* his disappointment. I could feel him thinking, *Why can't he ever do the right thing?* I could almost hear Dillon Deronda snickering, spitting out a sunflower seed.

C'mon, Hoscowitz, rip it. If Hoscowitz ripped it, I could just lope home, easy as pie, no responsibility.

Ping. Hoscowitz connected. "Ha! It's a fly ball! Ha!" Old Violet's voice came croaking out. Yup, it was a deep pop-up, all right. It soared up and up and up. Everybody watched it. Ten Gorillas, and nine Sharks.

Drop it, drop it, drop it, I was praying. *C'mon DROP it,* but Zack out there in the field called for it. His glove was up, his face was calm. *He* was going to be the hero, and not me at all.

But there was this other thing we had talked about in practice. *If there is a pop-up with less than two outs—*

The ball smacked right into that well of leather with a perfect little plop.

Gareth's voice seemed to reach my ears from a hundred miles away. *"Tag up, Willy, tag up, tag up."*

What? Tag up?

And then I remembered. *Tagging up.* It meant I could still run home. But I had to get there before the ball did, before the catcher could catch it and tag me.

Stop thinking, Willy, and DO it.

C'mon, I can move my feet; I'm not a goldfish, I'm a gorilla.

"Run home, Willy!"

Run home! The sax took off the same time I did. Those notes soared, and they pushed me along, they carried me. I was running home, all right, I was running home to the park, for the park, the park was my home, and Otto Pettingill was up there in his apartment playing for *me,* Willy Wilson. I stopped thinking about my dad, I stopped thinking about Rat-Face Dillon Deronda, and I just ran, flinging myself into a slide for the last two feet. I could taste the dust in my mouth as the catcher's glove hit my arm.

"Safe!" the umpire yelled.

And then the crowd was roaring.

"Gill Park Gorillas, Gill Park Gorillas, go-o-o-o-o-o Gorillas!"

I pulled off the mask. Sweat was dripping down my face. Dillon Deronda was throwing his glove on the ground, stamping his feet, gnashing his rat teeth. He wasn't a cool customer anymore at all. The game was over, and the Gill Park Gorillas had won.

twenty-eight

Some pieces of music, I like them so much,
I wonder why they have to end,
and if I had the strength,
I'd keep playing them forever.

—*Otto Pettingill*

And then I was face-to-face with my mother and father. My mother looked smaller, she had shrunk somehow, and then I realized why when she said, "My goodness, Willy, you've grown ten inches since you've been away."

"Well, maybe not ten," said my father, who liked people to be accurate with their facts, but then he smiled and slapped a hand on my shoulder. "But you *have* grown a lot. And you played a good game out there."

I waited, expecting him to say more, like, you should have done this or that, but he didn't.

"I didn't know you were coming," I said.

"You didn't?" Mom was surprised. She looked at Aunt Bridget, who waggled her eyebrows at me.

"Thought you'd like to be surprised," she said.

I nodded, grateful. Aunt Bridget had guessed that if I had known my parents were coming, I would have been a frozen gorilla. And as it was, I almost had been. The music had saved me, kept me moving.

"How about we take you out for a celebratory luncheon, Willy?" my father asked. "Where would you suggest, Bridget? Gloria's finest restaurant . . ."

But before Aunt Bridget could think of Gloria's finest restaurant, we saw Belle Vera, Mitch Bloom, Liesl, and Gareth walking toward us.

"Parents of the hero," said Mitch, putting a hand out to Mom and Dad. "A fine sturdy sapling, that boy of yours—going to grow into a fine oak or maple or towering evergreen one of these days."

"Such a plais-ure," said Belle, also giving my parents a warm handshake. "You must be so proud. He is the apple in your eye, *n'est-ce pas*?"

"So you're the parents," said Liesl, hands on her hips, studying them with a look that seemed to say she had never seen people like them before.

I nudged her with my elbow. "Don't stare at them like that," I whispered.

My mother began to blink, which is what she does when she's nervous, but my father surprised me. He bowed slightly and said, "That was some fielding out there. When that lout came sliding into third base, fully aiming to knock you flat, you just stepped aside, caught the ball, tapped him on the shoulder, and hiked it back to second—all neat as a pin. Did you see that play, Marcia?" he asked, turning to my mother. "Lotta strength in that little arm of yours," he said to Liesl with a chuckle. It was a real chuckle, not a grunt. "Speaking of arms, though, the pitcher of those Sharks—I've never seen a boy pitch like that; I've never seen a boy with such focus." I felt my stomach tighten. Wouldn't you know it, my father would be standing there praising Rat-Face Dillon Deronda. "Not a great personality, though," he added. "You can see that." I relaxed a little and breathed.

"This is the Gorillas' coach," said Aunt Bridget, putting a hand on Gareth's shoulder. "Gareth Pugh, the mastermind behind it all."

"A privilege," my father said, shaking his hand.

I caught Aunt Bridget's eye and smiled. I couldn't believe it. My father actually seemed to like my friends.

"You Harvey Pugh's son by any chance?" my father asked Gareth. Gareth nodded, and then by another chance, there was Harvey Pugh, walking toward us. My father broke into a huge smile and went right over to him and stuck out his hand and said, "Harvey Pugh," and Harvey broke into an even huger smile and shook his hand back and said, "Bill Wilson!"

"The infinite brother- and sisterhood of lawyers," said Aunt Bridget, and I couldn't help feeling pleased that my father and Gareth's father knew each other.

"Well, where does everyone want to go?" Aunt Bridget asked.

"I should think the children would like to shower and clean up before they go anywhere," Mom said.

Liesl looked at her and then at me and giggled. Then I saw her about to open her mouth, and I also saw Mitch shoot out his arm and put it around her shoulders.

"Good idea," he said. Liesl closed her mouth.

"And I," Belle Vera said, "I propose a peek-neek right here in the park that not so long ago was almost not a park, and I, who have no other responsibility, will prepare it all for you, no?"

"Oh, no, we couldn't—" my mother started to say, but Aunt Bridget spoke right up.

"That would be most kind of you, Belle," she said firmly.

"I shall see you at the fountain on the point of five o'clock," said Belle.

Mitch put a hand behind Liesl's back and steered her toward Aunt Bridget. "Take her and clean her up," he said to her.

"We'll go if we can tear my brother away from Harvey," Aunt Bridget said.

The two of them, my father and Gareth's father, seemed to have a lot to say to each other. I could hear them saying something about a lawsuit. They inspired me.

"Why do lawyers have to have such big closets?" I asked, turning to Gareth.

"I don't know," he said, looking at me with a slight frown on his face.

"They have to have room for all their law suits," I said.

Gareth paused a moment and then he punched my arm. "That's pretty bad, Willy," he said.

"Yeah, so bad you didn't think of it yourself."

"My dad *does* have a big closet—"

"Yeah, yeah, so does mine."

"Do you think all lawyers do?"

"We could do an investigation," I said. "Want to?"

"Yeah," he said. "How much more time do you have before you have to go home?"

"I'm not sure," I said. I suddenly had that brick-hitting-you-on-the-head feeling you get when you realize summer is on its way out and school is right around the corner. "Maybe a week."

"Maybe just enough to conduct a superficial investigation," Gareth said thoughtfully.

When we climbed up the stairs to Aunt Bridget's and opened the door, I saw that the apartment was spotless. All gorillas were gone, not just our uniforms, and for the first time since I'd been there, the worktable actually looked like a dining room table. Flora was tucked back into a corner. She was even wearing a suit. And Aunt Bridget must have vacuumed a thousand times. There was no sign of a single black hair—for that matter, there was no sign of Sophie. Mom looked halfway comfortable as she sat down at the table and actually accepted the tea Aunt Bridget offered her. Then Aunt Bridget offered Dad a beer, and I thought, *Aunt Bridget never has beer on hand. Boy, she really has made an effort!*

"How's the violin coming?" my mother asked.

"I'll play for you," I said.

"Oh," said my mother with a happy squeak of surprise.

I went into my room and brought out the case and opened it with two little clicks of the clasps. I took out the violin and tucked it under my chin. Then I started playing "The Park Song." It was the tune I had been working on. It had the fountain in it, with its changing colors, and the sunlight coming through the trees, and kids skateboarding, and Gareth yelling at a kid to steal second base, and I plucked the strings to make the *ping* of the bat contacting the ball. It had Old Violet with her socks all wrinkled down around her ankles, and Mitch Bloom in it, too, selling flowers, and Jerry Rabinowitz writing *green green green* as the fountain sent up its plumes of water. In one place it got loud, and that was supposed to be Mrs. Nugget's voice. In another place I played these minor chords—they were a little sour, like Dillon Deronda, but I figured I had to put in everything about the park, the good and the bad. And in other places I tried to be both soft and bright, like Liesl's chalk drawings on the pavement.

Of course when I played it, it wasn't that good. I could feel in my fingers how I wanted it to come out, but it wasn't getting into the bow or into the strings. A badly played violin is the worst sound in the world, and I knew it probably sounded ridiculous to my parents.

But I was thinking, *I don't care what they think, because this is for me.* I snuck a glance at them. They had sort of blank expressions on their faces, but at least they weren't plugging their fingers into their ears or throwing up or anything. I turned my back on them and walked over to the window. I was going to play for the park, like Mr. P. did every day, but just as I was about to start the tune over, I realized that Mr. P. wasn't playing.

With a pang of worry, I brought the violin down from my chin and held it under my arm and held my breath, listening carefully to be sure. No, there was that naked sound of the city without the music. A car honked, a truck rumbled by.

But then I thought, *He's been playing all day*. Playing the sax was probably hard on his lungs and he was probably winded—he had played so much and so well.

"Why, Willy, that was *wonderful!*" I realized my mother was gushing at me.

I turned to her and smiled. It was nice of her to try to be nice. "It wasn't really that great," I said, "but I'm working on it."

Then the phone rang. Aunt Bridget answered it. "Oh no!" Her voice rose and she quickly walked with the phone into the kitchen.

"Not bad news, I hope," said Dad.

I could hear Aunt Bridget say good-bye and put the phone down. She walked heavily into the living room and came over to me. She put her arm around me. "Willy," she said, "Mr. Pettingill is in the hospital. He had a stroke—"

I stood very still. Outside, a car came to a screeching halt and there was a blare of horns.

"Willy—"

I put the violin back into its velvety bed and I loosened the bow and put it back.

"Who called and told you?" I asked, trying to keep my voice steady.

"Belle Vera," she said. "She'd gone to his apartment to invite him to the picnic—she thought you'd like that, and he'd like that—and she found him. . . ."

I shut the violin case, *click, click,* snapping shut the clasps. My father was standing, watching; my mother was sitting, watching.

"I want to go to the hospital," I said.

"What is it?" Mom asked.

"Who is it?" Dad asked.

"Otto Pettingill, the owner of Gill Park," Aunt Bridget said. "Willy and he . . . became friends."

Dad was pacing, jingling the change in his pockets. "We'll all go," he said.

twenty-nine

That first summer I went to the park,
I found out I had a personality.
—Willy Wilson

The next few days passed in a blur. I woke up thinking about Mr. P. I went to sleep thinking about him. I tried imagining he was still in his apartment looking out his window, instead of lying in a hospital bed so sick he couldn't even recognize me. I kept trying to push away the thought that if he hadn't played the sax for our baseball game, he'd be all right now.

I asked permission to play my park song in the hospital room, because I thought it might make him well, but it didn't. Mr. Pettingill died on the third night after we beat the Sharks. He died at eleven-eleven P.M. Belle Vera said he probably chose that exact moment on purpose. She said he liked things like that.

There was a huge service in the park for him. I think hundreds of people came. I didn't think any of those hundreds of people was a member of his family, though. No brothers or sisters or kids or anything, although maybe he had cousins I didn't know about. Maybe all of us, the people of the park, were like his kids.

Tilly Willauer, the opera singer and Mr. P.'s old girlfriend, sang a song from a Mozart opera. Then the Gloria Symphony Orchestra played some of his favorite pieces. It was the most beautiful music I had ever heard in my life, and the saddest. It made me ache all over. Aunt Bridget, who was standing beside me, took my hand and held it. I was glad she was there.

Then the mayor of Gloria made a speech about how Otto Pettingill had a vision, and how his vision had made the city of Gloria one of the most unique and beautiful cities in the world. The service had begun just before dusk, so when it ended, the fountain lights came on, and the orchestra played the Mozart sonata Mr. P. always imagined should go with it. As I watched the colors changing, from red to green to yellow to blue, I thought about the fountain being Arethusa; and then I thought, the fountain wasn't Arethusa, it was Mr. Pettingill. It was his heart still beating, right in the center of the park. The thought lifted the ache out of me a bit.

When the music ended, no one said a word. I'd never been in a silent crowd of people before. They started to leave, alone or in bunches, spreading out all over the park, in every direction, north, south, east, west, still not saying a word. Pretty soon Aunt Bridget, Mom, Dad, Mitch, Belle, Gareth, Liesl, and I were the only ones left.

"Now what?" It was Gareth. The words came blurting out and his voice startled me. "What's going to happen to the park?"

Mitch cleared his throat, as if it was difficult to talk, and his Adam's apple bobbed. "I don't think we know," he said finally. "Unless Willy knows. Willy? You were probably the closest person to him in these last few weeks. Did he give you any inkling of his thoughts?"

I shook my head. "He only talked about how he didn't have any kids to leave it to."

"Well, we'll just have to wait and see," Dad said.

And then everyone was quiet again, wondering what was going to happen to the park.

The only good thing about the next few days was that Mom and Dad let me stay longer at Aunt Bridget's than had been originally planned. Dad said we could stay until I was ready to leave, and he and Aunt Bridget went for walks together and seemed to do a lot of talking. I was glad they were getting along. Even Mom didn't seem as stressed out as usual. She sat in the park with Belle Vera when Belle wasn't teaching Liesl, and she knit, because of course she could never just sit and do nothing. The best thing was that Belle kept telling her how wonderful I was, and how lucky she was to have a son like me, and Mom kept looking at me in a new way, as if she hadn't ever seen me before.

Two nights after the service, the phone rang. It was Gareth's dad, Harvey Pugh, and he was calling to tell us that Mr. P. had appointed him to be his new attorney and that he wanted me and my dad to come into his office the next day because he had something important to tell us.

When we walked into Mr. Pugh's office the next day, I had butterflies in my stomach, big time, even worse than when I was watching Dillon Deronda wind up for a pitch. I could tell something big was about to happen, just from the way Mr. Pugh was looking at me.

"Please sit down," said Mr. Pugh. "I am going to read sections from Mr. Pettingill's will that are relevant to you."

He started reading from a big sheaf of papers. It was about the park, how it was going to be run by a board of directors. Mitch Bloom was on the board, and he, Harvey Pugh, was on it, and a bunch of other people I didn't know, and then me, Willy Wilson. Me, I was going to be on that board.

And then, although he, Mr. Pettingill, didn't have a son, or a next of kin, he had found someone who would serve that purpose very well—and that was me. I, William Wilson, was to be the new owner of Gill Park.

I got so dizzy I had to lean against Dad, and Dad kept squeezing my knee and saying, "You've got big shoes to fill, son, big shoes to fill." But then he said, "And you *will*, Willy, you'll do a fine job." We spent about another hour in Harvey Pugh's office, going over things, a lot of which I didn't understand too well.

In the taxi, on the way back to Aunt Bridget's, I was thinking about the last taxi ride I'd taken with Mr. Pettingill. And then Dad said, "It's not your fault. It's not your fault Mr. Pettingill died."

I kind of reared back, looking at him. *How did he know?* How did he know I thought Mr. P. had had a stroke because he'd played the sax all day, when he could barely breathe, and he'd played it to help me play baseball?

"I thought," Dad said, without looking at me, "when my father lost most of his money, I thought it was my fault. I thought that for a very long time. Willy, you didn't make him smoke cigarettes all his life." He said it firmly, and a tightness inside me loosened up.

"I feel sad," I finally said. "I feel sad that I'd just gotten to know him and now he's gone."

"He lives on in this city," Dad said. "And the more you learn about his park, the more you'll know about him." He raised his eyebrows at me, his thick eyebrows, and for a minute he looked just like Aunt Bridget. I nodded, and I was glad he was who he was because I knew I was going to need someone who was smart and tough and practical to help me with the park.

"And what about getting home, now, Willy?" he asked.

"We can go tomorrow," I said. "I just want the rest of the day today, okay?"

"Okay," said Dad.

When we got back to the apartment, Dad told Aunt Bridget and Mom the news. Aunt Bridget sat at the worktable, flamingo material piled high around her. She turned as pink as the stuff she was sewing.

"My gosh, Willy," she said, shaking her head. "That is really something. Well, Mr. Pettingill was lucky you came here this summer, that's all I can say. We're all lucky."

Mom started to cry. She came and put her arms around me. "Oh my goodness, Willy," she said. "Oh my goodness."

"Maybe I'll make a big pool for the goldfish," I said. Mom pulled back and stared at me. I grinned at her. She was going to have a tough time with me. I had made a new goal for myself. I was going to try to make her laugh at least once a day.

And then we heard elephants stampeding up the stairs. Gareth and Liesl came bursting in. "C'mon, Willy," said Gareth. "You gonna sleep all day or what?"

"I wasn't sleeping," I said. "I—"

"Willy Wilson has holes in his head," said Liesl. "He forgot we had practice."

Aunt Bridget and my parents were looking at me. I shook my head. I wasn't ready to tell anyone I was the new owner of the park. It didn't even seem that real to me yet. I needed to live with the idea for a while.

"It's my last day," I said instead.

"Oh, bummer," said Gareth.

"But I still want to practice," I said. "If it's okay with you."

"Hey, would I say you couldn't practice just because you're abandoning us?"

"Yes," I said.

Gareth grinned. "Hey, guess what? Next time you see me, I'll have my braces off. Two more weeks."

"Wow," I said. "You'll be so good-looking, the girls'll faint when they walk by you."

"Yeah, right," said Liesl. "They'll faint all right, but not from his good looks."

I laughed, but the achy feeling was starting in my throat again. I'd miss these two characters, I really would. Everyone back home was so ordinary.

"Well, so, let's go," Gareth said impatiently.

"Listen, Willy, could you get me some things from Rosa's on your way back, one last time?" Aunt Bridget asked. A pink feather floated past her nose. She struggled with a piece of pink gauzy stuff that seemed to be jammed in the machine, and the ache settled in my throat.

"Christopher Columbus!" she muttered. "Who invented flamingos?"

I went into the kitchen and cautiously stuck my fingers into the money cup. To my surprise, I only felt the dullness of a wadded-up paper bill. From the living room, Aunt Bridget seemed to guess what was happening.

"I took the fishhooks out," she called. "In case you were wondering why you are no longer in danger of being impaled by lethally barbed pieces of wire."

I came back out to the living room with the twenty and looked at her. "Roger's inside me, you know," she said, concentrating on what was happening beneath her fingers. The machine seemed to be working again, and the pink stuff was gliding along under the needle. "I don't really need his fishhooks to stab me into remembering him."

I nodded. "I know," I said. I was thinking about Mr. P., how he was inside me, too.

"I've got something for you, Willy Wilson," Liesl said. She was standing next to Aunt Bridget, her hands behind her back. For Liesl, she was looking shyer than usual. She stuck out a hand and handed me a rolled-up piece of paper. I unrolled it and then just stared and stared. It was a picture of Mr. Pettingill playing the piano, not in chalk but in charcoal, so it was in black and white; but she had drawn notes rising off the piano, and they were all done in different colors of chalk. They were swirling all around his head, and then flying out the window. Outside, everything was still in black and white, except for the notes, until you got to the park, and she had drawn that in color, so the notes blended in with the colors of the park. It wasn't exactly realistic, because she'd squeezed a lot of the park in, so you could see everything, like the fountain and the statue of Colonel Pettingill, Mrs. Nugget's swimming pool full of kids, and the baseball diamond. She had all the team members on it, standing in position, with Aunt Bridget on the side sitting at a sewing machine making gorilla suits, and near it was the tree house, and Mitch's field of flowers, with Mitch and Belle perched smack in the middle of it drinking strawberry drinks.

Aunt Bridget pushed her hair back with one arm. Her eyes were full of tears. "Well," she said. "Liesl, that is one heck of a present."

"Just so you don't forget us or anything." Liesl spoke in a small voice.

"It'll be great to have it on my wall at home," I said, thinking about my boring bedroom. "And I'm not leaving forever, you know. I'll be coming back. A lot." I grinned. It was actually going to be fun to tell Liesl I was the new owner of Gill Park. She'd squeal a lot. "And you guys can come visit me," I added, although it was hard to imagine Liesl in my house, with its white rugs and the goldfish.

"For Pete's sake, Wilson," said Gareth, every inch of him vibrating. "You think we've got nothing to do all day but stand around and yack?"

"Yeah, get a move on, buster," said Liesl, pulling on her cap. She was wearing shorts and a T-shirt and looked mostly normal, but she hadn't wanted to let go of that tonsil-colored baseball cap.

I waggled my eyebrows, which, I had realized not long ago, were as thick as Aunt Bridget's—as thick as Dad's, too. It was one of the things we all had in common—a Wilson family trait.

"Well," said Aunt Bridget, waggling hers back, "I see that some things don't change."

"C'mon, we're outta here," Gareth said, pulling me by the arm. "See ya guys later," he yelled to everyone.

We ran across the street into the park. *Zap zap zap,* I could feel it—the electricity in the park was back. Zack Mack was playing the harmonica. He was whaling on it, playing crazy notes, zigzaggety notes; and Spiky Mike was having a party playing the bongos. It was a real racket that made you want to leap around and dance. Wow, it was great stuff! Yeah, Mr. P. would have been pleased.

We passed the statue of Colonel Pettingill and my skin prickled. Yeah, that statue made my skin prickle, and the benches and the birds and . . . and the *fountain*. I pictured, for the hundredth time, that moment in Harvey Pugh's office when Harvey Pugh read the will. Mr. P. wanted *me,* Willy Wilson, to keep all this going!

Now Gareth and Liesl and I ran past Mitch, and he saluted us with a pair of shears; and then we ran past Jerry Rabinowitz, who was bent over a notebook and didn't see us. Belle Vera was on another bench, feeding the birds whole-wheat crumbs. She blew us a kiss. We ran by a group of day care kids, who were mostly swinging on swings, their little voices rising up to blend in with the harmonica; but one little kid, all by himself, was dancing. He was jumping around, bopping his head, shaking his body all over.

And as we approached the baseball diamond— Toenail's hair stood out like a bright blue flower—we passed Old Violet's bench and her bony hand suddenly grabbed me. She held me in an iron grip for a moment, her eyes the only sharp thing inside all those wrinkles, and she croaked, "*Ha!* What a big boy you are, *ha!*" and then she let me go.